Praise for *How It Went*

"Lyrical, immersive stories about work, neighbors, and the land . . . Berry has that gift for entertaining amid serious intent, and the many lighter, very human moments in his elegiac, cautionary, wistful stories keep them from sinking into jeremiad without diminishing his message. A fine collection by an enduring, endearing master."

—*Kirkus Reviews* (starred review)

"Lovingly written . . . Taken together, the 13 chapters in Wendell Berry's *How It Went* create a tale that gently unwinds and doubles back on itself, not so much like a river but more like a flowering vine . . . Berry's prose—in *How It Went* and just about everything else he's written over his long career—is imbued with compassion . . . A book full of such gentleness, wisdom and humility seems preposterous in this day and age. It's also something of a miracle. We are lucky, in such times, to still have a writer like Wendell Berry."

—*BookPage* (starred review)

"New stories like those in *How It Went* add context, depth, and breadth to Port William. They tell us, once again, the kinds of work we can do to help mend a hurt world. Go read them."　　　　　—Ethan Mannon, *Front Porch Republic*

"Berry's stories effortlessly portray characters who feel as real as they do distant—members of a bygone era, of a harder yet simpler time when things revolved around real life, not the abstractions of our modern age. Despite being in the past, they are not simply 'products of their times.' Berry is careful to construct his characters as close to real flesh and blood as possible, illustrating that the virtues of stability, community, and a life well lived are as desirable and possible today, in any town or city, as they were and are in Port William . . . With a mix of good humor and piercing insight into the human condition, Berry examines the inner life of Andy Catlett—and a great deal more. Never forceful, Berry makes his points nonetheless. Andy is learning to navigate the challenges of a changing world, some times with more grace than others. Along the way, we can learn something too."

—Dr. Ryan Hanning, *Hearth and Field*

"Berry's humanity and clear-eyed intelligence steer the stories away from simple nostalgia and into a thoughtful analysis of how communities inevitably change over time. This accomplished author still has much to offer." —*Publishers Weekly*

"Many profound lessons are found in these nostalgic pages . . . Followers of the author's previous work will no doubt love this florilegium, but no doubt this anthology has something for everyone. A solid collection from a dependable author, for fans and nonfans alike." —*Library Journal*

How It Went

How It Went

Thirteen More Stories of the
Port William Membership

WENDELL BERRY

COUNTERPOINT
Berkeley, California

This is a work of fiction. All of the characters, organizations, and events portrayed in this novel are either products of the author's imagination or are used fictitiously.

Copyright © 2022 by Wendell Berry

All rights reserved under domestic and international copyright. Outside of fair use (such as quoting within a book review), no part of this publication may be reproduced, stored in a retrieval system, or transmitted in any form or by any means, electronic, mechanical, photocopying, recording, or otherwise, without the written permission of the publisher. For permissions, please contact the publisher.

First Counterpoint edition: 2022
First paperback edition: 2023

The Library of Congress has cataloged the hardcover edition as follows:
Names: Berry, Wendell, 1934– author.
Title: How it went : thirteen more stories of the Port William membership / Wendell Berry.
Description: First Counterpoint edition. | Berkeley, California : Counterpoint, 2022.
Identifiers: LCCN 2022023035 | ISBN 9781640095816 (hardcover) | ISBN 9781640095823 (ebook)
Subjects: LCGFT: Short stories.
Classification: LCC PS3552.E75 H69 2022 | DDC 813/.54—dc23
/eng/20220516
LC record available at https://lccn.loc.gov/2022023035

Paperback ISBN: 978-1-64009-615-8

Cover design by Lexi Earle
Cover art © iStock / CaptureLight
Book design by Wah-Ming Chang

COUNTERPOINT
2560 Ninth Street, Suite 318
Berkeley, CA 94710
www.counterpointpress.com

Printed in the United States of America

1 3 5 7 9 10 8 6 4 2

This book is for Den—who defined my task:
"How to remember, and why"

—and for Billie

Contents

CONTENTS

How It Went

The Divide

(V-J Day)

Andy Catlett is sitting on top of a post in the board fence between the back yard and the barn lot, ringing the dinner bell. He can hear the sound of it, dong after dong, flying away, rippling out in circles over the countryside, how far hearable he does not know.

He is facing westward, the now-fading sunset on the horizon beyond the Bird's Branch hollow, and the world beyond, known to him only from maps in a geography book: California, the Pacific Ocean, its many bloodstained islands now quiet, and finally Japan that now to his supposing also is quiet. Distances and events that he cannot imagine are yet somehow present to his thoughts. In a thought that he will think for the rest of his life, he is sitting at the world's center, sending forth in circle after circle around him the joyous clamor of the bell. It is August 15, 1945, and he is ten days past eleven years old.

———

Before supper he had been in the barn, leading and handling the filly foal of old Rose, his grandpa Catlett's saddle mare. By portions of intuition and perseverance and portions of incomplete advice from his grandpa—"Don't fight her. You can't force her to agree with you. Mind, now, what I tell you"—and some help gently given by Dick Watson, he broke the foal to lead with a halter that Dick had fashioned for him from a piece of cotton rope. But now he had a real leather halter of his own, made by A. M. Naparilla in his harness shop at Hargrave. "That's a Naparilla," his grandma said of the halter as she presented it to him on his birthday, announcing the name, rare and famous in that country, as another kind of woman in a different place and time might have said, "That's a Botticelli." For the little halter was in fact a thing of beauty, a work of art, as the boy himself readily saw, though he did not know yet to call it "art." Before he ever put it on the filly, he spent much time handling it and looking at it, seeing and feeling its lightness and strength, the elegant proportions of its supple leathers finely stitched, its shined brass hardware, its precise fitting to its purpose.

That evening, when he had returned the mare and foal to their pasture and started to the house for supper, he had heard suddenly rising and building in the town of Port William, too far away to be ordinarily heard from, an exuberation compounded of car horns, bells, and a shout compounded of many voices.

And so he ran the rest of the way to the house, to be met on the screened back porch by his grandma, whose eyes were moist behind her glasses, who said, "Oh, honey, it's over. This terrible war has stopped at last."

The public electric line by then had reached their place. She had heard about V-J Day on the small radio she had ordered from the catalog.

She was not a woman of high expectations. That human beings would by their sorry nature make war did not surprise her. She had been born when memories of the Civil War were still fresh, and she had borne, grieving in her thoughts, the wars that had followed, surprised by none of them, and yet knowing, as a woman of her kind and time would know, the cost in suffering and tears. And so when she spoke the word "war" she invariably added the adjective "terrible," as if to call it almost courteously by its full name. She applied the noun, moreover, not to a series of similar but distinct calamities, but rather to a single calamity that, as she expected, reappeared from time to time. In her grandson's memory of her, her sentence of just before the Christmas of 1941, "Oh, Andy, what of this terrible war that has come upon us!" seemed merely to continue in the summer of 1950: "Oh, Andy, we are at war again. It has come again."

Falling so short as he did of her length of memory, Andy

supposed only that the peace he had awaited with longing had finally come. So far as he was capable of feeling, he felt that it had come forever.

With the clamor from town still audible through the open windows by the kitchen table, he was not long at his supper. His grandmother, greatly moved by her thoughts, only picked at her food. His grandpa, by long habit concentrated on the place, its life and its work, conceded by principle, perhaps by defiance, no importance to the largeness of the world. While his grandma picked and lingered, gazing away, and his grandpa ate as ever with intense concentration and relish, Andy placated his hunger by cleaning up his plate as fast as he could. He then pushed back his chair and ran out again into the yard. The tumult at town was still in progress and he had to respond. He climbed onto the post-top and, seizing the bell rope, began ringing back to Port William and to all the world.

Without a thought of anything else in the world he might do, he rings the bell. In his little knowledge and great ignorance, he rings back to the celebratory ruckus in Port William and with a fierce gladness in his heart for the end of war and the beginning of peace. He will not forget his simplemindedness of that night, which joined him as if drunkenly to the equally singular elation that danced, drank, shouted, and sang itself away before dawn in Port William. He rings for the peace he dreams has come forever, for all the absent ones who now will come safe home.

That all who have gone will not come back, he knows, though in his joy, in the flightiness of his young mind, he is not thinking of them. He knows that his uncle Virgil, his mother's brother, whom he loved and loves, who was reported "missing in action," is now believed by the family to be dead, killed in what way, somewhere along the battle lines of the Bulge, they will never know.

Of such knowledge he knows more. He knows that his uncle Andrew Catlett, the loud-laughing, careless, unreckoning man whom he loved and loves, for whom he was named, was shot dead in a quarrel at Stoneport, several miles upriver from Port William, in the summer before.

Andy's experience thus, at the beginning of his twelfth year, includes grief. It includes, intermittently for the time being, but also forever, awareness of the curtain, impenetrable by the living, before which they enact their lives. He has begun his acquaintance in the graveyard on the hill at Port William, a fellowship that by now, when he is old, far exceeds his acquaintance among the living.

He does not know the deaths that are to come, that will end his childhood. He has not begun the long growing up that will call him to the work that will be his to do.

He does not know the wars yet to come.

That his government, in ending the war, has again proved the willingness of some of his kind to do anything at all that is possible, he has after a fashion heard, but is far from knowing.

He is far from knowing that, virtually from that moment of rejoicing at the coming of peace, an industrial assault upon his home community and countryside, and upon such homeplaces everywhere, will now begin, and will continue into his final days.

And so ring the old bell, young Andy Catlett. Ring your ignorant greeting to the new world of machines, chemicals, and fire. Ring the dinner bell that soon will be inaudible at dinnertime above the noise of engines. Ring farewell to the creaturely world, to the clean springs and streams of your childhood, farewell to the war that will keep on coming back.

A Conversation

(1943–2013)

Andy Catlett's grandma and grandpa Catlett had survived the hard times of their life—the depressions of the 1890s, the first decade of the next century, the 1920s, the 1930s—and had held onto their farm by a series of tight squeezes. This surely amounted to success, as the people of their kind and time and place would have reckoned it, but it was a success that rested upon a long discipline of economic minimums. They survived by the plentitude of their subsistence, which they took from their farm by their own skill and effort and that of their one or two hired helpers who shared in the same providence from underfoot, but they survived also by much abstention from the economy of money, much doing with less and doing without.

One of their luxuries at the time of Andy's childhood was the coal pile in the barn lot from which they fed the large stove in the living room. Loaded with coal at bedtime, the stove gave warmth all night and quickly enlarged its radiance in the early morning. For the large iron cooking stove in the kitchen, wood was both a cheaper fuel and more versatile. Thick pieces of a heavy, long-burning wood such as hickory were fine for winter; in summer, lighter woods in smaller pieces burned quickly, to cook a meal without too much heating the kitchen.

And so, also in the barn lot and not far from the coal pile, there was a woodpile. The coal pile, which never changed except by getting bigger or smaller, was of no interest to Andy. But the woodpile was always changing. It was a work place, a place of transformation, and to Andy it was a place of never-ending interest. Some of the happiest times Andy spent with his friend Dick Watson were at the woodpile. Dick was Grandpa Catlett's hired hand who belonged, as Andy knew, to the race once enslaved and still subservient in that country, but who in Andy's consciousness had emerged from his race and "place" completely as himself.

The trunks of trees would be gathered as they blew down or were felled in the woods or the fencerows, hauled to the woodpile, and ricked on the far side of the sawbuck and chopping block. To replenish the supply of firewood for the kitchen, the logs or poles would be lifted one at a time off the rick, placed on the sawbuck, and then sawed into stove-lengths, which either as splits or rounds would be piled on the near side of the chopping block to be carried as needed to the woodbox beside the kitchen stove. To split the larger chunks, Dick stood them or leaned them against the chopping block and drove his axe into the grain with hard, precise licks. The chopping block would be a substantial log that would be slowly chipped and fretted away as the axe struck through. Finally the thinned-down chopping block also would be laid onto the sawbuck and sawed into firewood. Except for the sawdust and the smallest chips, everything that went into the woodpile would be burned.

This work was ceaselessly varied. No two logs, no two poles, no two sawed chunks were ever alike. Each was a problem to be solved. Every pole, for example, had to be correctly placed on the sawbuck so as to lie steady under the saw. Every one of the larger sawed chunks presented a best place for the axe to strike, where the grain and the knots gave least resistance to the blade.

From time to time Andy would make a secret attempt to use the axe, but he lacked both strength and accuracy. As the men of the place would have told him, the work was above his breakfast, and he could not hit where he looked. But from the age of eight or nine, he was able to take one of the handles of the two-man crosscut saw. And this he had longed to do. The saw was sharp, its teeth well set, and Dick could use it by himself when he had no help, as he usually did not. He would stand erect in a sort of stopped stride, drawing the saw through the deepening kerf and pushing it back in short strokes with the skill and the perfectly submitted patience that the task required. But to Andy the unmanned handle seemed always to be asking him to take hold. And finally when he had become tall enough, or perhaps only eager enough, he took hold.

And then he began to learn the job. It was not as simple or as easy as it had looked. He learned first that his help could be a hindrance. If he pushed the saw, as in his wish to help he was much inclined to do, the blade warped and bound in the kerf.

And Dick would say, for a while he had to say too often, "Don't push the saw, buddy." Or, "Pull, but don't push."

If he bore down on the saw at his end, thinking to make it cut faster or just from weariness, that made it pull harder at Dick's end.

And Dick would say, "Don't ride the saw, buddy."

Riding the saw could be maddening for one's partner. People forbore to ride the saw for fear, as Andy would later learn when, as a bigger boy, working then not with Dick Watson: "If you're going to ride, pick up your goddamn feet!"

But back then, in those old times at the woodpile, in his great patience, his endlessly tried and unending gentleness, Dick only said, until he seldom needed to say again, "Buddy, don't ride the saw."

When he worked at the other end of the saw, Andy wanted, as much almost as he would want his supper, to believe he was helping Dick, and perhaps he was when he worked well. He knew he was helping when Dick went to the kitchen with a big armload of stovewood and he followed with a smaller one.

Andy loved Dick Watson with his whole heart, and so it was fortunate for him that Dick was a man entirely honorable and upright. At that time Andy was far from the consciousness by which he might have formed and articulated a judgment, but he probably would not have loved Dick so much if he had not also looked up to him. His love was in large part a response to Dick's kindness, but a part of it also was his admiration for Dick's workmanship. He could see, when it was pointed out to him by his grandpa or his father, that Dick was a good workman, but Andy also was capable of seeing it for himself. Perhaps he was not always competently aware of what he was seeing, but it would have been plain to him that Dick knew how to work. He did not fumble at it. He never applied too much or too little force, but always just enough. He was never angry or violent in applying himself to a task or a problem. He was not a slacker. He did not hurry. Surely Andy would have loved him less if he had ever seen him slight or shortcut his work.

And Dick was one of the few teachers in Andy's childhood that he did not at some time resist or resent. This certainly was because he loved and respected Dick, but it was also because they were chiefly friends. Dick taught Andy what he needed to know when he needed to know it. If Andy was determined to help saw the wood for the kitchen stove, then obviously he needed to know how to use the saw, and if he was going to learn, Dick would have to teach him, and Dick did. It was the same when Andy begged to drive the team of mules, Beck and Catherine, that were known as Dick's team, and Dick finally handed him the lines. It was best for both their sakes then that Andy should handle the lines and speak to the mules in the right way.

"Tighten up on 'em, buddy. Not too fast. Take hold of 'em."

At first when Andy would be turning the team, Dick would sometimes have to tell him quickly, "Not too short! Not too short! Straighten 'em up a little."

And sometimes Dick would need suddenly to overrule whatever Andy was doing: "Whoa!" It was wonderful how instantly the mules obeyed when Dick spoke.

If Andy's blunder had been large enough, perhaps dangerous enough, Dick would laugh out in ridicule and relief that it had not been worse. "Oh ho! You asking them to do what they know better than." When he saw that the mules concurred in Dick's bad opinion, Andy would feel three times embarrassed.

He was most seriously scolded one day when, as he saw, Dick was truly frightened for him. He was riding his grandpa's saddle mare and he had urged her into an all-out run, which in the first place he had been forbidden to do, but then he rode her without slowing, hardly tightening the reins, straight over a steep bank. When he rode on back to where Dick had stopped his team, he met a stricture he had not expected or even, until then, known to expect.

"I *saw* what you did. She'd a stopped, the way I thought she might, you'd have kept right on, right over the top of her head. Long way to the ground, buddy. Would've hurt."

He took thought then. He looked at Andy with a surprising, terrible gravity, for he had imagined what the boy had not. He said, "I reckon you don't want to get *killed*. I reckon I don't want to *see* you get killed. Oh ho, buddy, no *sir*!"

It was a moment, for Andy, of startling seriousness—a startling perhaps endearment, though he would never know what to call it. Dick had required him to imagine what he had risked, and he had imagined it. He knew two things. He knew he would not take at least that particular risk again. And he knew that the gravity of that brief time belonged only to the two of them. There would be no need for either of them ever to speak of it to anybody else.

And so their friendship was intimate insofar as they had acknowledged a seriousness in it to each other and to nobody else.

Endearments enough passed to Dick from Andy, whose mind then was unbalked and freely spoken. They may have passed the other way too, but from a mind by then, by its history, far more complicated, and old Andy, in strict courtesy to Dick and in hope of justice, allows himself no conclusions.

And yet he wonders. Dick had of his own flesh no child. Did Andy in some way perhaps stand in for Dick's never-existing actual son or grandson? "Well," he thinks, "it is best to wonder and not know."

It was a long conversation, long at least from the boy's perspective, an eight-years-long conversation, kept up almost ceaselessly when they were together by Andy's inexhaustible wanting to know, his always wanting to take part, and Dick's enduring willingness to respond. Often Dick responded at length, remembering and describing in detail, because of the pleasure of being so intently listened to, or because of his own interest in what he had to say.

As he needed to, Dick instructed Andy in how to work, how to stay out of the way of somebody who was working, how to be careful. But sometimes he would turn the conversation to less welcome instruction. This would have to do with growing up, becoming responsible, and taking the right kind of care of things. Dick, it seemed, had looked ahead and seen, as the boy Andy did not wish to see, Andy Catlett as a grownup man with obligations and responsibilities. Perhaps Dick, in his good heart, felt for the boy the burden of that coming time and the burden of the boy's unreadiness, and he assumed the duty of trying to warn him and somehow prepare him. He would hold up the example of Andy's father, who was responsible, who had accepted the burden of the care of things:

"I was with your daddy the other day, helping him get up the cattle, and, never mind what else, he was always looking about, always fixing something, always picking up something, putting it away."

Andy saw, though only feelingly, that Dick Watson, who had few things of his own to take care of, was in that way a freer man than Wheeler Catlett, who certainly had more things to take care of than Andy had, or wanted ever to have. Andy very much did not look forward to such a growing up, and Dick's lessons did not ease his mind.

But Andy's predicament, as he may also have seen feelingly, was more complicated than that. From the example of his father as a responsible man, as that example was understood and offered by Dick Watson, Andy reacted fearfully and strongly in favor of his childhood, which was his freedom from grownup responsibilities and, in his unobstructed friendship with Dick, freedom even from the burden of his own racial history. And yet his whole motive in his conversation with Dick was his persistent wish to outgrow the ignorance and smallness of his childhood. He wanted to participate. He wanted the adult knowledge and skill and strength that would permit him to take part with Dick as Dick's equal, using the world's fundamental tools to do the world's fundamental work.

In his old age, looking back, Andy is amused to think how much they talked—hurrying along to keep up with

Dick, he would have to stop his talking or asking just in order to breathe—and how varied were their subjects. Because Dick was a grownup and an elder, it never occurred to Andy to doubt him. He knew, Andy assumed, the answers to all questions. If they had been given the time, if they could have lived on at the same ages forever, Andy might finally have asked them all. And Dick might have provided answers—right or wrong, it would not have mattered.

Old Andy is touched to the heart by the freedom of their talk. Then, though they spoke as man and boy, they seemed to speak otherwise as peers. When other people, especially other grownups, were present, reminders of the racial, the burdening and bewildering, difference would be present. In the freedom, the freedom at least for Andy, of their own conversation, with the whole outdoors around them, no observers, no mirrors, anywhere, Andy never thought of either of them as a representative of any category. He thought of them only as who and where they were.

And now, in an age of categorical politics and categorical manners, when actual faces and lives fade from sight beneath the smears of mechanical abstractions, old Andy is turned back from his thoughts repeatedly to the question, What shall I call him? What thought-word, in speaking of him to those who are now young, shall I use to signify his race and his part in history? In his own day, if he had to be identified by category, Dick would have wished to be called a

"Negro," and white people of good will would so have called him. He would have been hurt and insulted, then, to be called a "black," which he would have taken as equivalent to "darky." If he had been called an African American, he would have been as bewildered as Andy would have been to be called a European American.

In his thoughts Andy returns repeatedly to the name Dick Watson, by which he cherished and still cherishes the man in his time and place, as he recognizes and cherishes, wonderingly, by his own name the boy who was Dick's companion then and there. As they stand together in his memory, as frail and yet perhaps triumphant as his memory is, the encasements of oversimplification shrivel and fall from them.

And so they are at the woodpile. It is a cold, sunshiny late fall afternoon. Dick lifting the heavy end, Andy the light, they have laid a long locust pole onto the sawbuck and rightly balanced it. Andy is working at his end, so he has claimed, of the long saw. He is, as against his wish even he knows, still a small, skinny boy, but he thinks he may have grown a little and got a little stronger over the summer. Almost without having to think about it, he is not riding the saw, he is not pushing it. He is almost afraid to tell himself that he is doing it right, but he is doing it right. The saw has been newly sharpened and set. You can hear its sharpness in the clear, clean-edged sound of it, singing through the hard wood. It runs lightly, almost floating through the kerf, but biting in, biting in, the bright sawdust spewing to either side, until another stove-length drops onto the pile at the end of the sawbuck.

A Clearing

(1945–2014)

Andy Catlett remembers a day when he was wandering. He does not remember very surely when this was. He was a boy, young enough to be glad his elders did not know where he was, old enough to allow the foldings and unfoldings of the countryside around Port William to draw him into wandering. It was early summer. Perhaps school had just ended after using up so many months of the year, and he was feeling free.

He remembers where he was. He was, at the beginning of this memory, crossing one of the more distant ridges on his grandfather Feltner's farm. He was at the top of the ridge. When he looked back to where he had started, he could see, among the treetops of Port William, the steeple of the church, one of the gables of his grandparents' house, and the cupola on the roof of their home barn. On the top of the spire on the top of the cupola, though he was too far away now to see it, he knew that a mockingbird was likely to be singing.

Ahead and below, in the direction he was going, the open pasture ended and the woods rose up, its various greens all darker than the grass of the pasture. Perhaps he was thinking of the shadow contained in the woods, where he would be out of the sun. In that direction he could not see far. It was maybe a hundred and fifty yards to where the woods started, or resumed, and at that distance the mottled greens and shadows of the foliage against the strong morning light appeared as impenetrable as a wall. Above the woods was only the sky with its wide procession of white clouds. Behind and below him now lay the wooded hollow he had just climbed out of, his steps seeming to assume a direction as he entered the full sunlight and could see his shadow on the ground.

He walked anyhow fairly straight and purposefully down to where the slope steepened and the woods began again. As he approached the woods, it lost the aspect of a wall and acquired increasingly articulate shallows and depths, revealing ways in. He began to see openings, high up, that birds might fly through.

He found an entrance lower down, along the brushy edge, where he could go in himself, and he went in. A great change of feeling came over him, as complete as the shadow of the woods within the woods. In the open grassland of the ridgetop, it easily could seem to him that he watched himself, as if from somewhere above, as if from a cloud, and he could easily tell himself, as he often was likely to do, the story of himself: "Now the boy is walking across the ridge."

In the woods he disappeared from himself, or he disappeared from his picture or his vision of where he was. In the woods his vision was all of the woods. In the shade of the woods he could see better, and he was cooler. Though he had not noticed or thought about it, the direction that had guided him across the ridgetop now had left him, and he began again to wander. He could not see far ahead, and he had no direction in mind. Or he had lost whatever direction he might have had in mind, or any need or wish he might have had for a direction. It was too soon after breakfast, too long until dinner, for him to be hungry. His shadow when he had been in the sun was still plenty long. Nobody anywhere would be expecting to see him for a long time. When his shadow would be maybe about as long as he was tall, when the day began to heat up even in the shade, when his stomach notified him that it was getting empty, then direction would return to him, and he would head back toward his granny's kitchen. But time also was lost to him now. He was in no hurry.

And so he became almost thoughtless. He had already submitted, almost without thinking, to the charm of the little paths that laced across the face of the slope under the trees. It would be maybe fifteen years before there would be deer again in this country. Here and there he would see and for a while walk along a cow path. But most of the paths, and about all of them where the slope was the steepest, had been pressed into last year's fallen leaves by the feet of small animals. These were just traces, almost invisible, and yet offering dependably the best footing. Sometimes they led to something he saw that he wanted to get closer to and see better. Sometimes they led to or departed from the mound of earth at a groundhog hole. Once he stopped to look at a half-grown gray fox that had stopped to look at him, and a shiver crawled up between his shoulder blades.

Earlier, when he had sat down on a large tree trunk that had fallen against a standing tree, providing both a seat and a backrest and was thus a good place to sit, not to be wasted, he had happened to sit still long enough to see two young squirrels at play. And he thought then about the .22 rifle he planned to have when he got old enough to be allowed to have one. He would be a skilled hunter. He would be a good shot. He would become the sort of young man who would be modest about his ability to bring home food of his own getting.

But when he saw the fox he did not think of his rifle. The fox looked at him intelligently and curiously, as perhaps he looked at the fox. The fox was perfect in its features, its coat, and the alertness of its ears and eyes. Andy's fear that he would scare the fox hardly amounted to a thought, but it was strong and it held him so still that he felt a little stiff and strange when he began again to move. When the fox, having seen as much as it needed or wanted to see, vanished quickly but all the same unfrightened and without haste, Andy felt curiously complimented, as if the fox had agreed to his presence in the woods. He felt more present than he had been before. And now he walked with conscious care to be quiet.

The paths led him in slants upward and downward along the face of the bluff. Sometimes he lost a path. It would seem just to disappear, though he knew enough to suspect that its disappearance was a failure of his eyesight, but then he would find soon that another or the same one seemed to offer itself to his lifted foot. He was most alert and most pleased where the ground was steepest. He could imagine himself a mountain climber then, proud of finding footholds that permitted him to walk upright on ground as steep as a ladder, only once in a while having to catch hold of a bush or a sapling or a handy vine. Where the ground crumbled and slid under his feet, he would have to put out a hand and walk three-legged. In one place, very satisfactorily perilous, he had to go four-legged and sideways until he had his feet firmly beneath him again. He felt in his flesh then, as if remembering, the advantages of a small animal with four legs.

In a while he followed one of the paths up again to where the slope gentled, and again he walked easily without thinking of his feet and hands. He had come to a height of ground, which lay in fact at the farthest extent, the "point," of the ridge he had crossed earlier. Here the ridgetop itself was wooded because just here the ground began a downward slant at about a right angle to the slope he had been following. He had never before come so far. He had never been here before. Ahead of him presently the woods lightened and opened, showing more and more of the sky. He worked his way through a somewhat brushy edge to a wire fence, old and rusted but still stock-tight, where the woods abruptly ended and a grassy pasture began.

He was looking down into a small, open valley shaped like half a bowl. The slope of the hollow of it was grassed all around up to where it steepened and was again covered by trees. "It is a clearing," he thought. He liked the word "clearing," which he associated with the farms of the first settlers, which he imagined opening slowly in the forest around a small house built of logs. There was no house in this clearing, which he might have regretted but did not, for the place seemed complete in itself as it was. At the bottom of the valley, at the end of a pair of wheel-worn tracks through the grass, there was a barn and a small shed. A split-rail fence, one of the last of its kind, formed a lot in which animals might be penned. The two buildings probably had never been painted, but had weathered to the silver gray of old poplar siding.

The clearing, of perhaps twenty acres, was filled with light, the scale of it close and intimate, as if scooped out by the hands of somebody who loved the shape and feel of it. The year's first growth of grass lay upon it, impeccably green, visibly fresh and new, and yet, visibly also, the result of years of work and care. Already, because he had now grown up enough, he had begun to hear his father when he said, as he often had and would, "This land responds to good treatment." And he had watched and seen enough already to notice that this place was neat. There was no disorder, no leftovers lying around. Any tools or materials worth keeping had been safely put away under the tin roofs of the barn and shed.

The whole place within the surrounding woods had the character of hand-making and hand-cherishing. It had an ordinary, modest beauty that belonged entirely and only to itself. He did not say to himself that it was beautiful. He felt, he recognized, the beauty of it in his flesh, as he had felt the presence of the fox and the perfection of it.

For no reason he can remember, for no good reason at all, he never went back to that place. That he had only happened upon it in his wandering made his encounter with it both an accident and, because he would belong ever after to his memory of it, a part of his fate. Perhaps because he did not need to see it again, he never saw it again. Later and in scraps, as his way of learning went, he would learn the name and something of the story of the man whose place and work it had then been. He was Alvin, yet another of the Coulters who had rooted and branched in the Port William neighborhood until, by some of the families they had outnumbered, they were considered as prolific as bean beetles.

In his day Alvin Coulter was famous around Port William for his hard work and hard drinking. He was a man too reckless of himself, too demanding of others, too hard to please, too finally alone to live to be very old. But while he lived and was strong, the beautiful little valley was his work, one of the ways he had found to offer himself to this world.

Alvin's life and Andy's overlapped by only a few years. Though the two of them probably shared a kinship somewhere in the long cross-branchings of the Port William family trees, and though in the regardlessness of his childhood Andy no doubt passed many a time under the gaze of Alvin, he does not remember ever seeing him. And Alvin was long gone by the time Andy was old enough to hear and remember pieces of the sort of legend that for a while survived him, and to figure out that the little valley belonged to Alvin's farm that lay mainly in the bottomland along the river.

Now, in his latter years, Andy knows that the clearing in the woods could not have lasted as he saw it for very long. And by this he understands how fragile it was, how temporary and passing, in the rush of the terrible century in which he and it had so briefly and so lastingly met. For he has never forgotten it. He could not have forgotten it.

That day, until his stomach informed him that it was empty, he stood without moving, his hands on the top strand of the fence, looking with all his might at the beautifully kept small place that was surely one of the first landmarks or measures of his conscious allegiance, that would never again be far from his thoughts, that no doubt had influenced every right decision he had ever made.

One Nearly Perfect Day

(1946)

Because he was not free to farm every day, Andy Catlett's father had a way of thinking up, of foreseeing in detail, farm jobs for his boys on days when they were out of school. And thus, even when they were as young as eight or nine, Wheeler Catlett granted to his sons the freedom that he had denied himself by being responsibly employed. Sometimes they were capable of the work he gave them. At other times the "little jobs" he had thought of would not turn out as he had supposed, but would take all day and would involve much difficulty or frustration or even failure. What he had conceived as a freedom would become involuntary servitude and a trial.

As inheritors of their father's freedom, or of his visions of what he might have felt free to do if he had been his own son, Andy and Henry learned to anticipate his "little jobs" with doubt, sometimes with dread. But one of the jobs he gave Andy turned out so splendidly that Andy was as delighted as he was surprised. Wheeler would have been surprised too, if Andy had ever told him.

One of the fences at the home place, after many repairs, had at last become useless. The wire was rusted through and brittle, and the posts were rotten. The crop year was beginning, and none of the regular hands of the place could be spared. To take out the old fence, Wheeler had hired the only available help: two of Hargrave's semi-employed jacks-of-all-trades, who in their abundance of spare time were faithful historians of public life from the vantage of the shady benches in front of the courthouse in the summer and from several indoor points of view in the winter.

It was not a long fence. The job, Wheeler rightly thought, ought to take no more than a day. It would be a trifling job that would clear the way for a new fence to be built when experienced hands would have the time. Or that was the explanation Wheeler gave Andy. Later Andy would suspect his father of contriving the project to focus the often-wandering mind of his son by a dose of responsibility.

"Andy," Wheeler said, "I've hired Dingus Riggins and Les Stout to take out that stretch of fence I showed you. I've told them what to do, and now I'm going to tell you."

His father's drift was plain enough, and Andy caught it.

Dingus and Les were not to be depended on to remember exactly what Wheeler had told them. It would be Andy who would have to remember.

"They'll have to take the wire loose from the posts," Wheeler said, "and roll it up. Some of the posts have broken off. The others I think they can pull up. But they'll have to dig around some of them, maybe pretty deep. Take a log chain and the spud bar and the other digging tools. They're to load the wire and the posts on the wagon and put them in the sink hole. I'll have Snazz harness Beck and Catherine before he goes to work. They'll be in their stalls."

And then Wheeler's voice became even more precise and cautionary. "Now listen. You're to stay along with them, remember what they're to do in case they *don't* remember, and help them a little if they need it. You understand?"

"Yessir," Andy said. And he did understand. He understood the job and how it was to be done. And not then but later, he understood that his father was sending him not just to remember but to be a witness and, imaginably, an informer. With Andy there, the job would get done in one day. Otherwise, it would take two.

Andy was staying with his grandma, pretty conscientiously filling the place of the man of the house after the death of his grandfather. He had finished his morning chores and his breakfast and was waiting at the barn when Wheeler drove in with Dingus and Les, each with his lunch in a paper sack. For drinking water, Andy had filled a jug at the well. He had also loaded the digging tools, a log chain, a hammer, and a pair of fencing pliers onto the wagon, ready to go.

When Dingus and Les had got out of the car and were standing with Andy in the barn door, Wheeler said, "All right. You fellows know what to do. Andy here will go with you to show you the fence."

"We got it," Dingus said.

"Yes, *sir*," said Les.

"You know what to do," Wheeler said to Andy.

"Yessir," Andy said.

And then abruptly, as his way was, Wheeler was heading back out to the road, the atmosphere of the place palpably altered by his departure.

"Now this here boy," Les said to Dingus as if Andy were not present, and though he knew perfectly who Andy was, "he would be Mr. Catlett's son? Am I right?"

"This here would be young Mr. Andy Catlett," Dingus replied. "He is Wheeler Catlett's boy. Or, anyhow, he was caught in Wheeler's trap. And he is supposed to show us where is what and what is where. His daddy said."

And then, turning to Andy, Dingus began again. "Now,

young Mr. Catlett, your daddy said you would know where this team for us to use is."

"Yessir, Mr. Riggins," Andy said. "I'll get 'em for you."

He went to Beck's stall and brought her out. "If you'll hold this one, please, Mr. Riggins, I'll get the other one."

Andy noticed in passing that he was having perfect manners, and he was pleased. He went to Catherine's stall, brought her out, and stood her in her place beside Beck. And then occurred a small crisis that would have a large influence upon all the rest of the day.

Having by his better knowledge made the team available to them, Andy was prepared to defer to the two men who, as grownups, he expected to take charge of him, the team, and the job of work. There was a critical moment when they should have done that, when it was up to them, or one of them, to do that, but they allowed the moment to pass. If they were going to take charge, they should have attached the check lines to the bridle bits of the two mules, driven them out of the barn, and hitched them to the wagon that waited, loaded with the tools, in plain sight in front of the corncrib.

They did nothing. They seemed to have abandoned the field of adult authority. Andy felt this a social embarrassment that he needed to put an end to. And so he detached the lines from the mules' hames, shook them out, snapped them to the bits, and then, sensing again that the initiative had been left to him, he stepped behind the team and picked up the lines.

By then he was nearly twelve years old. He had not only watched the experienced teamsters and under their supervision taken the lines into his own hands during most of his life, but he had even been allowed on his own to work a team at a few simple jobs. And so he knew what to do. He spoke to the mules and drove them out to the wagon. He backed them into their places on either side of the tongue.

"This here boy," Les said, "he ain't hardly no more than weaned, and he's a teamster?"

"Aw, that boy's a teamster!" Dingus said. "He's a driver! Ain't you seen him handle them mules?"

"I seen! I seen!" Les said. "Yeah, I seen!"

At that time Andy was still supposing that Les's first name was spelled with two s's.

Beck and Catherine were knowing and dependable. Andy had been cautioned more than once not to argue with them "because they know their business better than you do."

Wheeler had designated the old team for that job, as Andy even then understood, not because the two mules could be entrusted to Dingus and Les, but because Dingus and Les could be entrusted to the mules.

Dingus did go so far as to help Andy hitch the trace chains to the singletrees. "Drop two links," Andy told him. But then Dingus hoisted himself up beside Les on the edge of the wagon bed and dangled his feet. Clearly there was nothing for Andy to do but take the lines.

He drove the team out of the lot and back through the fields, first Dingus and then Les opening and shutting the gates as they went through.

When they got to the place of their work and Andy stopped the team, Les said, his tone suggesting that they had already accomplished a great deal, "And now what's *next*?"

"Why," Dingus said, "we're a-going to take out that there fence."

"And how are we a-going to do that?" Les seemed to suggest that they would have to do so by some method not yet invented.

"Why, we're a-going to start at this here end here and go to that there end yonder."

Confronted with yet a further vacancy of authority, Andy finally recognized what a day this was. Not only was it going to be up to him to be the teamster, and under the authority of no grownup. It was going to be up to him to run the whole show. Or so he concluded, and so it went.

Later he would be obliged to wonder if the show had not been run, in fact, by Dingus. Perhaps by more subtlety than Andy had given him credit for, Dingus had employed Andy for that day to do a lot more work than Wheeler had expected him to do, though Dingus paid for this probably by a harder day's work than he had intended for himself. Andy would come eventually to meditate at some length on the possible difficulty of distinguishing between stupidity and low cunning—and, for that matter, between stupidity and certain kinds of intelligence.

Owing to whatever cause, Andy had the upper hand of that day. He was free to work a team of mules, to work himself, to manage the work of others without, for once, the intervention of higher authority. Such a day, he knew, was not likely to come to him again, not maybe for a time longer than he had so far lived, and he now became cunning himself in order to safeguard his authority. It was a fine, bright day, neither too hot nor too cool, and Andy exerted himself to keep anything bad from happening in it.

Assuming again his extremely good manners, he said, "Mr. Riggins, if you please, sir, you could knock the staples out of them posts, and I'll help Mr. Stout to roll up the wire."

And Dingus said, "Yes, *sir*, young Mr. Catlett."

And so it went. They did the work in stages: loosening and rolling up a section of wire, working the still-standing posts out of the ground, loading wire and posts onto the wagon, hauling them to the sinkhole. The decision as to when and how much to load the wagon was, each time, left to Andy. Otherwise, he ran the show only by staying at work himself and thus keeping the other two at work. The rest of the bossing was done by Dingus. At each step of the work, no matter how many times they had already done it, Les asked how to do it, and Dingus told him. Les was the man with the questions, Dingus the man with the answers. Otherwise, their talk was devoted to speculation, very instructive, upon Andy's future transactions with girls, to memories, equally instructive, of similar transactions committed by themselves, and to elaborations upon what they would accomplish if they were vouchsafed a new beginning at the age of this here boy.

At the approach of dinnertime, signaled by the whistle of a dependable train as it raced through Smallwood, three miles across the fields, they returned to the barn. Andy unhitched and unbridled the mules, watered them, and gave them their ration of corn. Dingus and Les sat on the well top, the freshened water jug between them, and opened their lunch sacks. Andy went to the house where Grandma Catlett had his dinner ready. She also had ready some comments that she had meditated upon for several hours.

"That's a fine pair of strays your daddy has brought here

to put you to work with," she said as she took the pan of hot biscuits from the oven and put two on each of their plates. She said, as she always did, "Butter 'em while they're hot."

And then she said, "Common as pig tracks! I knew 'em before they were born. They're nobody for you to be associating with. I don't know what your daddy's thinking about. Nothing, I reckon."

It was strange, her way of speaking of Wheeler at times as if he were no older than Andy. And then Andy sometimes would take up the strange duty of defending his father to his father's mother, as if she were the mother merely of another boy.

"I imagine they were the best he could find," Andy said. "Somebody's got to do the work, and they're working right along. We'll get it finished today."

She said, "Psssht! I reckon!"

And then she said, "Well, let *them* do it. You keep where you don't have to listen to 'em."

Andy thought, "Too late!" But he said, "Well, somebody's got to drive the team."

"And that's got to be you, I reckon! Nobody ever heard the like!"

When Andy got back to the barn, Dingus and Les were sitting propped against the water trough, legs flat before them on the ground, their heads wobbled over, dead asleep. This was another social embarrassment. Andy did not have the seniority or standing that would have made him eligible to wake them up.

He knew how Rufus Brightleaf would have handled the situation. Rufus would have shouted out, "*Off* your ass and *on* your feet!"

And then when they needed to be humored past the jolt of that waking and back into the mood for work, Rufus would have said, "Stay with me, boys! First thing you know, you'll be living in one of them penthouses, plenty of good drinking whiskey, couple of old ladies about twenty years old to keep house for you. You'll have it *made!*"

But Andy could only go to Beck's stall, bring her into the light of the big doorway and shout "Whoa!" too loud, though the mule, knowing what to do, had already stopped. And then he brought out Catherine, again shouting "Whoa!" as she also was stopping in her place.

"Ain't that that damned boy back at it again?" Les asked.

"Aw, that's that boy back at it," Dingus said. "That boy's a *driver!*" He grunted as he got to his feet. "Oh! Lordy Lordy Lord!"

They went back to work then. The afternoon proceeded about as the morning had. By a reasonable quitting time, even somewhat earlier, they had finished the job.

To Andy's great relief, his father had not shown up to see how they were getting along. He was not going to show up until quite a bit later, when he would drive up to where the three of them were standing in the barn door. He would be in one of his better moods.

"Well, boys. How did you get along?"

And Dingus would reply in a tone of authority, "We got her done," implying that, contrary to Wheeler's expectation, they might have accomplished a great deal more, if only they had had it to do.

"Good! And Andy here, did he earn his keep?"

Indulgently, as an adult commending a child, Dingus would say, "When we needed help, that boy give it. He was right there. Aw, Mr. Wheeler, that there is some boy."

Dingus's tone, in fact, was worse than indulgent. It was patronizing—implying that if Andy had not been in the way the work would have been easier and faster.

But Andy's freedom of that day lasted as long as he needed it to. He drove the team and wagon and the two passengers back to the barn. As far as Dingus and Les were concerned, their day's work had been completed, and so once more Andy alone unhitched the mules, did up their lines, unbridled them, watered them, put them in their stalls, and gave them their corn. Though he was small for his age, he could have unharnessed them, but not, he knew, with the proper grace and dignity, and so he left the unharnessing for Snazz Goodall when he would come in from his own day's work.

Except for that slight defect, Andy now had his day of running the show intact behind him. It had been one of the best days of his life. It was ever to be one of the best days of his life. After that day, he would work again under the supervision of grownups. Again, leaving the thinking and authority to them, he would make mistakes or shortcut a job and be reprimanded. He would have a lazy spell, and he would shirk. He would be absentminded. He would revert, that is to say, to being a boy. But he had made that one day good, had satisfied himself, from start to finish.

When he had completed his obligation to the mules and come to stand in the doorway with the other two, Les said, "Now this here boy, ain't he a fair hand, not to be nothing but a pup?"

"You got it," Dingus said. "You seen it through. This here boy's liable to grow up to be a ramrod of a lawyer like his daddy."

"Now that Wheeler Catlett, he's a right smart of a lawyer, am I right?"

"You're right!" Dingus said.

And then Dingus offered a revelation that astonished Andy then and for a while afterward.

"Aw, that Wheeler's a hoss pistol! Like I say. Anything you can think of, he's got the words for it. I seen him one time defending this old boy had got into a little shooting scrape. Wheeler claimed he was really a good boy, had just made a mistake, and they ought to go light on him and give him another chance. When the jury got up to go out, Wheeler told 'em, 'Remember, boys, there's a little black-eyed mother up there in Heaven, watching what you do!' And he just *cried!*"

"How you reckon them lawyers can cry the way they do?"

"Aw, they just go without pissing about three weeks."

It had been a splendid day, a sort of crescendo in Andy's childhood. And it was a day that he would grow into as adult knowledge and understanding grew in his mind. He would come to see that it was only the latest war and the consequent shortage of good farm hands—a shortage that would be permanent, and ever worse—that could have brought his father to consider Dingus and Les as possibly more than detachable pieces of courthouse furniture. And in due time he would locate the peculiar poise and confidence of those old workmates in their perfect assurance that being white was an accomplishment.

Though Andy was hardly a "good boy," in those old days he had granted to adult authority a credit almost superstitious. And Dingus, as a self-appointed historian of the courthouse and teller of its tales, spoke with perfect Dingusian authority. Andy saw clearly the vision of his father pleading with the jury, which at the time he had become old enough to

imagine but never had imagined before. As to Dingus's eluci-
dation of the lawyerly mystery of tear-storage, Andy withheld
complete faith even in the moment. Later he grew to enjoy it,
and he has enjoyed it ever since.

A Time Out of Time

(1947–2015)

The old man, Andy Catlett, does not believe that the mind of any young creature is a blank slate. But he knows without doubt that young Andy Catlett, through the years of his boyhood, was being formed. He was being in-formed. He was being shaped, and this was his dearest education, as a creature of his home place, his home country, by his growing knowledge of it. He was sometimes deliberately taught by his grandparents, his parents, and the other elders who in one way or another were gathered around him. He was learning by their example, instruction, and insistence the ways of livestock, of handwork, of all in the life of farming that would make him, beyond anything else he might become, a countryman. But he was also shaping himself, in-forming himself, by knowledge of the country that he got for himself or that the country itself impressed upon him.

In the winter, Grandma Catlett occupied a room in the Broadfield Hotel down in Hargrave. And then, early in April, when Elton Penn came in his truck to load her and her spool bed and her bureau and her rocking chair to take her home, Andy would load himself and his bundle of clothes and books and go home with her. As he thought, as she allowed and maybe encouraged him to think, because probably it was true, her ability to live at home depended on him. He took a deep pleasure in the sense of responsibility that filled him then, and he was steadily dutiful and industrious. Grandma was cooking as always on the woodstove, and in the mornings, sometimes all day, they still needed the kitchen fire for warmth. Andy kept the kitchen supplied with firewood. When the cow freshened, Andy did the milking, night and morning. When they planted the garden Andy opened the ground in straight small furrows with the hoe, Grandma dropped in the seeds, and Andy covered them.

On schoolday mornings, after he had done his chores and eaten breakfast, he got himself out to the road in time to catch the school bus. But he had a little initiative in this. Because he was considered an occasional or temporary rider of the bus, he apparently was not officially expected by the driver. And so if he got to the road ahead of the bus, he would put up his thumb. If he failed to catch a ride, then he rode to school on the bus. This was a freedom he cherished, and he told nobody about it. The people who gave him rides also apparently kept his secret. He shirked his lessons, antagonized his teachers, stored up trouble for himself. On days of no school, as long as he showed up for meals, did his chores, and kept out of sight of the house, he was free.

On the warm afternoon of a Saturday in the early spring of 1947, when he had fished his way from pool to pool down Bird's Branch and had caught nothing, he came to a large, dry flat rock. He propped his fishing pole against a tree and lay down on the rock. The rock was unusually large and flat and smooth, and he felt that something should be done about it. And so he stretched out on it for some time, looking up into the treetops of the woods. He was no longer on the home place then, but had crossed onto the more or less abandoned back end of a farm that fronted in the river valley. He was at the mouth of a tributary dell known as Steep Hollow, whose slopes you could hardly climb standing up. The woods there was an old stand of big trees. Whether because of the steepness of the ground or the fragile benevolence of neglect, it had never been cut. But now, remembering it, he is obliged to remember also that a few years later it was cut, and is forever gone.

The woods floor was covered with flowers, and the tree leaves were just coming out. Andy's eyes were quick in those days, and he could see everything that was happening among the little branches at the top of the woods. He saw after a while, by some motion it made way up in a white oak and not far from the leafy globe of its nest, a young gray squirrel that, except for its tail, appeared to be no bigger than a chipmunk.

The squirrel was just loitering about, in no hurry, and Andy studied it carefully. The thought of catching and having something so beautiful, so small, so cunningly made, possessed him at once and entirely. He wanted it as much as he had ever wanted anything in his life. He knew perfectly that he could not catch a mature squirrel. But this one being so young and inexperienced, he thought he had half a chance.

The tree was one of the original inhabitants of the place. It had contained a fair sawlog in the time of Boone and the Long Hunters. By now it was far too big to be embraced and shinned up by a boy, or a man either, and its first limb was unthinkably high. But well up the slope from the old tree was a young hickory whose first branch Andy could shinny up to, and whose top reached well into the lower branches of the oak. Andy was probably a better than average climber, and he had spent a fair portion of his life in trees. He was small for his age, and was secure on branches too flimsy for a bigger boy.

He went up the hickory and then into the heavy lower limbs of the oak. The climbing was harder after that. Sometimes he could step from one thick limb to another up the trunk. Sometimes he had to make his way out to the smaller branches of one limb, from there into the smaller branches of the one above, and from there back to the trunk again. Finally he was in the top of the tree, a hundred or so feet from the ground. Just above him was the little squirrel, more beautiful, more perfect, up close than it had looked from the ground. The fur of its back and sides was gray, but to think "gray" was not enough. When he looked at it steadily and long, as his desire bade him to do, a wreath of light and color seemed to surround it. The fur of its underside was immaculately white. Its finest features were its large, dark eyes bright with intelligence and the graceful plume of its tail as long as its body.

Andy knew with a sort of anticipatory ache in the insides of his hands and fingers what it would feel like to catch and hold this lovely creature and look as closely at it as he wished. He climbed silently, and slowly from one handhold and foothold to another, up and out the little branches that held him springily and strongly until he was within an easy arm's reach of the squirrel. He reached his hand almost unmovingly out until it seemed almost to touch the squirrel. His hand seemed to him to offer a tenderness so welcoming that the squirrel might give itself into his grasp. Instead, it leapt, he felt, almost from his fingertips suddenly and easily to another branch. It did not go far, but the small branch it was now on belonged to a different limb from the one Andy was on. And so he had to go back to the trunk and start again. As he climbed he watched the squirrel with a curiosity as palpable and pressing as hunger.

About the same thing happened a second time. The almost-catchable little squirrel waited, watching Andy with a curiosity of its own, until it was almost caught. This time it ran a little farther out on its limb and leapt onto a branch of another tree, another oak. Now Andy had to climb a long way down to find a limb that crossed to the second tree, make his way out to limbs still affording handholds and footholds, limber enough to lean under his weight until he could catch a limb as strong in the other tree, swing over, go to the trunk of that tree and up and out to the highest branches, where again he almost caught the squirrel.

That was the way it happened so many times he lost count. It was as if he were being led by the hand with which each time he reached out. It was as if his hand itself incarnated his desire, and it foreknew or forefelt the squirrel's shapeliness and warmth, the breath and pulse of the life of it. And the squirrel seemed to wait, watching with interest, imaginably even with amusement, taking its rest, while Andy laboriously made his approach, and then at the last second, without apparent fear, seemingly at its leisure, leaping beyond reach, never far, but always too far to be easily approached again. In fact, Andy and the squirrel must have been at about the same stage of their respective lives: undoubting, ignorant, fearless, curious, happy in the secret altitudes of the treetops and the little branches, neither of them at all intimidated by the blank blue sky above the highest branches, the outer boundary of both their lives.

It was a time out of time, when time was suspended in constant presence, without past or future. It began to move again only when the squirrel finally leapt to the snag of a dead tree and disappeared into an old woodpecker hole.

And then it was late in the day, past sundown, and Andy was still high up among the tall trees. He had not thought of getting back to the ground for a long time, and from where he had got to he was a long time finding a way. The trunks were too large to grip securely and were limbless from too high up. He finally made his way to a grapevine, and slid down it slowly to ease the friction on his hands and legs. When he stood finally on the ground again, it seemed at first to rock a little as if he had stepped down into a boat. He was sweating, his hands and arms and legs bark-burnt and stinging, and he was a long way from home. He recovered his fishing pole, now divested of its old charm, and started home.

When the screen door slammed behind him and he stepped into the back porch, his grandma opened the kitchen door.

"Where," she said, drawing the word out, "on God's green earth have you been?"

"Fishing," he said, which was true as far as it went.

But he was late. He was too late. It was getting dark. In coming back so late he had betrayed not only her trust but his own best justification for staying out there in the free country with her and not in town.

"Oh," he said, "I'll go milk right now. I'll hurry. I won't be long."

She said, "*I* did it."

So: While he had been up in the treetops with the squirrel, unknowing the time of day, she, she alone, had done the evening chores and milked the cow. She said no more. She left him, as she would have put it, to stew in his own juice, which he did. He would not forget again. He would not forget the way he had learned his lesson.

Nor would he forget for the rest of his life his happiness of that afternoon. What would stay with him would not be his frustration, his failure to catch the squirrel, but the beauty of it and its aerial life, and of *his* aerial life while he tried to catch it among the small, supple branches that sprang with his weight as if almost but not quite he might have leapt from one to another like the squirrel, almost but not quite flying.

He had not wondered how, if he had caught the squirrel, he would have made his way back to the ground. It would take him several days to get around to thinking of that. The heights of that afternoon he had achieved as a quadruped.

From where he had got to he could not have climbed down with his two feet and only one hand while in the other holding the squirrel. If he had caught it, he would have had to let it go.

One of Us

(1950)

Grover Gibbs in his day and strength was no doubt the head philosopher-king of Port William. His only competitor for that "position," as Mr. Milo Settle called it, would have been Burley Coulter. But during Burley's often absences, for reasons known and unknown, from the Port William conversation, Grover would be faithfully present and presiding. He had not been elected, and he had no power. He presided by his presence, the excellence of his own talk and telling, and his insatiable relish of the wondrous world of Port William and its never-failing supply of stories worth telling. His preference in subject matter, hardly rare among the philosophers, ran in general to the funny and in particular to the ridiculous.

Port William's most productive source of the ridiculous was the prepotent tribe of Berlews, who, through several generations, had brought forth a succession of acts and exploits always surpassing the expectations of their most astute observers and historians. But there was also the even larger tribe of what Grover called the Ridiculers, whose entirely democratic membership extended to all who were qualified, including prominently himself.

It had been he, after all, who to make a drinking hole for his cows in a frozen pond, and not quite sober, had stood on the designated square of ice while he chopped all around it with his axe—a story that would have remained untold had he not told it.

And it was Grover who in all innocence, one night in Jayber Crow's barber shop, suggested to the young man known as Woger Woberts, for his pronunciation of his name, that he and his wife, Sassy, needed to get started on some children—to receive, as if by divine intervention, Woger's thereafter famous reply: "Ain't no use plantin' 'em one night and wootin' 'em up the next."

Grover received this and other such offerings as gifts to be thanked for, rightly appraised, and gathered into memory as provision against times of need. It may be that he presided over the dialogues of Port William also because of the remarkable character of expectation in his face, his eyes always alight with watching, his lips pressed lightly and firmly together as if in readiness to laugh and in readiness to restrain his laughter. And yet there was something more in his countenance that I saw only after I had grown fully into my own inheritance of the membership of Port William and the shared knowledge that made us friends after the fashion of a younger man with an older one. I could see in his eyes and his demeanor then the presence of a knowledge, far from laughter, of this world's loves and losses that I suppose he had revealed fully, and then perhaps inadvertently, only to Beulah, his wife. There was in his face, anyhow, a power that informed anybody who needed to know that he was not a superficial or a simple man.

Because he was not a superficial or a simple man, his assessment of the various Ridiculers and their doings seemed to consist at once of judgment, amusement, and forgiveness. Likewise, though in different degrees, there was a forbearance and a considering sort of decorum among most of the Port William men who gathered and talked in front of the stores in the summer shades or around the wintertime stoves. The town's never-resting amusement at itself was always reined back somewhat scrupulously short of either condemnation or glee. They were well known to themselves and one another, as they knew themselves they knew that they were known, and each knew how he and each of the others stood in the ranks of the Ridiculers. I once heard Grover say, after a burst of perhaps too much merriment at the expense of one of the Ridiculers, "Well. He's one of us."

By the grace of such knowledge, they responded with full appreciation, but also with a thoughtful complexity of reserve, when Laz Berlew, working as a carpenter's hired man in the very midst of the conversation and commerce of Port William, having sawed rapidly through a board, remarked with a knowing shake of his head to the inevitable audience: "I always like to cut my boards good and short. If you cut 'em too short, you can always splice 'em. If you cut 'em too long, ain't much you can do about it."

They granted a similarly circumspect delight to Cocky Berlew, who, on the occasion of the birth of his first child, beckoned the doctor aside to tell him, "Anything you want to know, you ask me. She ain't got no education"—and again when, on his reappearance in town after the birth of his eleventh child, they asked him, "Well, was it a boy or a girl?" and he replied, "I dog if I heard 'em say."

Not probably the funniest story that Grover knew, but the one he most enjoyed telling, involved two Ridiculers, and it took place, not in the intimate neighborhood of Port William, but just outside its farthest verge, down on the river road about halfway to Hargrave.

At that in-between place, fifty or sixty years ago, there was a small house just a few steps off the road with the woods grown up all around it. At some time long ago that house must have had the brightness and fragrance of new lumber, but nobody living could remember it new. Now it was far gone in the direction of the ground beneath it. As if in preparation for the fate of all natural things, the boards and battens of its outer walls had achieved about the color of the topsoil of the woods. A strong wind way back in the past had caused it to lean, as some might have said, somewhat alarmingly away from its chimney so that the chimney and the peak of the gable on that side were parted by maybe two feet. It had a number of patches, scraps of wood or tin, scabbed on to the surfaces of the boards. A small pane of one of its mullioned windows had been replaced by what appeared to be a wadded fragment of an old quilt.

In and about the middle of the last century this house was inhabited by two men whose average age, Grover said, was somewhere between thirty and sixty. Before they had happened upon so civilized a dwelling, also according to Grover, they had been living way off up Woodcockers Branch in a big hollow sycamore. To the ever-observant talkers up in Port William they were known as the Squatly brothers. They looked enough alike to be brothers, whether they were or not. Their appearance seemed, in that era, to be as unchanging as that of the house, and to harmonize, as you might say, with that of the house. Their clothes were similarly tattered and crudely patched. Their hair and whiskers appeared to have grown to a length of ideal dishevelment and then to have given up.

In times of good weather the two Squatlys were usually to be seen sitting side by side in a porch swing that swung from a front porch roof so near to collapse that Burley Coulter had seen fit, he said, to purchase life insurance policies on the occupants. In a more enlightened time such as the present, the Squatly brothers would be thought to live below "the poverty line." But of any need they may have had they gave no visible sign. They did not even look at the road. To those of us who passed from Port William on the way to Hargrave and from Hargrave on the way back to Port William, they appeared to be merely permanent. They clearly were Ridiculers but not of the kind normally produced in Port William.

Because we now have progressed so far from the "post-war world," and from memories of the still fully living Port William of that time, I must interrupt my story here to supply some facts of history.

A Packard, once upon a time, was a luxury automobile, a superior sort of outer garment, meant to recommend its wearer to the Heavenly Host. This vehicle was known in Port William mainly by reputation, but Port William knew its reputation very well. That is the primary fact.

A related fact is that in the years of his life from the time he began stepping out until his children grew up and left home, leaving it emptied of all but himself and Beulah, and he began to drive used pickup trucks, Grover Gibbs owned a succession of used cars still more or less usable, each of which, as a joke partly on himself, partly on anybody dumb enough to ask, he called "a small Packard."

A further fact is that in those bygone days, advertisements in various comic books and magazines offered the opportunity to send off a coupon, which would make the applicant a salesman of such portable articles of commerce as magazine subscriptions, garden seed, curative soaps, salves, and ointments. These offers, I believe, were aimed mostly at boys, who would not, as suggested, become rich, but who would likely be able to embarrass family members and neighbors into purchases individually trifling that might gather into untrifling profits. I myself spent several weeks selling magazine subscriptions in order to win the most valuable of the offered prizes: a "projector," consisting of a bright red tin box, a mirror, a lens, and a light bulb, which would enlarge upon a wall anything of a certain size that you wanted to "project." Because perhaps of its redness in its photograph, I thought it the most desirable thing I had ever desired. The thing itself, after thirty minutes, had about the charm of an empty bottle. Other boys, more charitably motivated and less gullible, peddled Cloverine Salve, a remedy commonly present in the households of grandparents.

And so there came a rainy morning when Grover Gibbs was on his way, in the small Packard of the moment, down the river road to Hargrave to take a mess of roasting ears to his landlady, the imperious and always somewhat amusing rich widow Mrs. Charlotte Riggins La Vere, but also to see who-ever might be seen in the hallways of the courthouse and other places of leisure, and to wonder at whatever wonders might be revealed.

Since just before daylight, little showers had come and gone, as if the sky were making up its mind finally to rain in earnest. When Grover had left home it had rained just enough to excuse him for taking the day off. But when he had got well down the road, as if to grant him a full justifica-tion, the sky got serious and sent down upon him and all the surrounding river valley a cloudburst backed by a hard wind. "All of a sudden," he would say later, "I couldn't see from home plate to first base." He reined the small Packard to a proper crawl, straining to keep sight of the road.

Before long, at first ghostly and then solidly in the strife and fume of the downpour, there appeared one of the Squatly brothers, walking. His head was drawn down between his shoulders, leaving just enough of it stuck out to wear the old felt hat whose waterlogged brim appeared to have flapped down over his eyes. "I don't reckon he could see hardly any farther than his feet," Grover said. "And there he all of a sud-den was right in front of me, and not much off to the side either. If I'd been one of these hot young bucks, driving the way they do, I'd have run right over him."

And so Grover eased past him, giving him plenty of room. And about as suddenly as the rain had come, a crisis of conscience fell upon Grover. How would *he* feel, afoot in such a storm, if some bastard dry in his car drove right past him and went on? But as small Packards went, this one was pretty nice. Beulah was enjoying it. And what would be the harm to it if he let this Squatly come sloshing into it shedding water like a downspout?

But his conscience piped up then, and it told him that if he didn't stop and do the right thing he would not be able to look in a mirror for the rest of his life. He said to his conscience that he didn't care if he never saw another mirror for the rest of his life. In the flower of his youth he had some-times gone out of his way to look in a mirror, but he was now safely past that.

Anyhow, he stopped. He even backed up several feet, see-ing as he looked back that the Squatly brother was coming at a run. But again Grover had to stop, for the rain, that he had thought could not get worse, got worse. It was as if a big lake of water in the sky was coming down all of a piece, at the same time driven horizontal by a wind stout enough to carry rocks.

The whole blast and gush of it was funneled in by the door as soon as the Squatly brother yanked it open. The small Packard might as well have dropped off of the Har-grave bridge into the river.

But the Squatly brother did not get in. Instead he leaned in, ignoring the storm, extending to Grover a small yellow-and-blue cardboard box. "Do you want to buy some Cloverine Salve?"

Grover decided to kill him. And then he decided to laugh. He put his head back and laughed. He laughed and let the rain fall and the wind blow.

"Naw, I don't reckon I do. But God bless you anyhow, old bud."

Dismemberment

(1974–2008)

It was the still-living membership of his friends who, with Flora and their children and their place, pieced Andy together and made him finally well again after he lost his right hand to a harvesting machine in the fall of 1974. He would be obliged to think that he had given his hand, or abandoned it, for he had attempted to unclog the corn picker without stopping it, as he had known better than to do. But finally it would seem to him also that the machine had taken his hand, or accepted it, as the price of admission into the rapidly mechanizing world that as a child he had not foreseen and as a man did not like, but which he would have to live in, understanding it and resisting it the best he could, for the rest of his life.

He was forty then, too old to make easily a new start, though his life could be continued only by a new start. He had no other choice. Having no other choice finally was a sort of help, but he was slow in choosing. Between him and any possibility of choice lay his suffering and the selfishness of it: self-pity, aimless anger, aimless blaming, that made him dangerous to himself, cruel to others, and useless or a burden to everybody.

He would not get over the loss of his hand, as of course he was plentifully advised to do, simply because he was advised to do it, or simply even because he wanted and longed to do it. His life had been deformed. His hand was gone, his right hand that had been his principal connection to the world, and the absence of it could not be repaired. The only remedy was to re-form his life around his loss, as a tree grows live wood over its scars. From the memory and a sort of fore-knowledge of wholeness, after he had grown sick enough finally of his grieving over himself, he chose to heal.

To replace his lost hand he had acquired what he named contemptuously to himself his "prosthetic device," his "hook," or his "claw," and of which he never spoke aloud to anybody for a long time. He began in a sort of dusk of self-sorrow and fury to force his left hand to learn to do the tasks that his right hand once had done. He forced it by refusing to desist from doing, or to wait to do, anything that he had always done. He watched the left hand with pity and contempt as it fumbled at the buttons of his clothes, and as it wrote, printing, at first just his name, in letters that with all his will it could not contain between the lines of a child's tablet. With two fingers of his pathetic left hand he would hold the head of a nail against the poll of a hammer, and strike the nail into the wood, and then, attempting to drive the nail, would miss it or bend it, and he would repeat this until he cursed and wept, crying out with cries that seemed too big for his throat so that they hurt him and became themselves an affliction. He was so plagued and shamed by this that he would work alone only where he was sure he could not be overheard.

To drive a stake or a steel post, he would one-handedly swing the sledgehammer back and forth like a pendulum to gain loft and force, and then strike. At first, more often than not, he missed. This was made harder by the necessity of standing so that, missing, he did not hit his leg. For propping, steadying, and other crude uses, he could call upon the stump of his right forearm. To avoid impossible awkwardnesses, he shortened the handles of a broom, a rake, and a hoe. From the first there were some uses he could make of the prosthetic device. So long as he regarded it as merely a tool, as merely a hook or a claw or weak pliers, he used it readily and quietly enough. But when some need forced him to think of it as a substitute for his right hand, which now in its absence seemed to have been miraculous, he would be infuriated by the stiffness and numbness of it. Sooner or later—still, in his caution and shame, he would be working alone—he would be likely to snatch it off and fling it away, having then to suffer the humiliation of searching for it in tall grass or, once, in a pond. One day he beat it on the top of a fence post as if to force sentience and intelligence into it. And by that, for the first time since his injury, he finally was required to laugh at himself. He laughed until he wept, and laughed again. After that, he got better.

Soon enough, because spring had begun and need was upon him, he put his horses back to work. By wonderful good fortune, for often until then he would have been starting a young pair, he had a team that was work-wise and dependable. They were six-year-olds, Chris and Nell. Andy's son, Marcie, who loved the horses and was adept at using them, was in this twelfth year then and could have helped. But Andy could not ask for help. His disease at that time, exactly, was that he could not ask for help, not from either of his children, not from Flora his wife, not from his friends, not from anybody. His mode then was force. He forced himself to do what he required of himself. He thus forced himself upon the world, and thus required of the world a right-of-way that the world of course declined to grant. He was forever trying to piece himself whole by mechanical contrivances and devices thought up in the night, which by day more often than not would fail, because of some unforeseen complication or some impossibility obvious in daylight. He worked at and with the stump of his arm as if it were inanimate, tying tools to it with cords, leather straps, rubber straps, or using it forthrightly as a blunt instrument.

In the unrelenting comedy of his predicament he had no patience, and yet patience was exacted from him. He became patient then with a forced resignation that was the very flesh and blood of impatience. To put the harness on the horses was the first obstacle, and it was immense. Until it is on the horse, a set of work harness is heavy and it has no form. It can be hung up in fair order, but to take it from its pegs and carry it to the horse's back involves a considerable risk of disorder. Andy went about it, from long habit, as a two-handed job, only to discover immediately, and in the midst of a tangle of straps, that he had to invent, from nothing at all that he knew, the usefulness of the prosthetic device, which was at best a tool, with an aptitude for entangling itself in the tangle of straps.

When, in his seemingly endless fumbling, he had got the horses harnessed and hitched, he became at once their dependent. He could ask help from no human, but he had to have the help of his horses, and he asked them for it. Their great, their fundamental, virtue was that they would stop when he said "Whoa." When he dropped a line or had too many thoughts to think at once, he called out, "Whoa!"

and they stopped. And they would stand in their exemplary patience and wait while he put his thoughts and himself in order, sometimes in the presence of an imminent danger that he had not seen in time. Or they would wait while he wound and rewound, tied and re-tied, the righthand line to what was left of his right forearm. A profound collaboration grew between him and the horses, like nothing he had known before. He thought finally that they sensed his need and helped him understandingly. One day he was surprised by the onset of a vast tenderness toward them, and he wept, praising and thanking them. After that, again, he knew he was better.

His neighbors too, knowing his need, came when they could be of use and helped him. They were the survivors, so far, of the crew of friends who had from the beginning come there to help: Art and Mart Rowanberry, Pascal Sowers and his son Tommy, Nathan Coulter, whose boys by then had grown up and left home, and Danny Branch, usually with one or two of his boys, none of the five of whom ever would stray far or long from the Port William neighborhood.

The first time they came, to help him with his first cutting of hay, their arrival afflicted Andy with an extreme embarrassment. He had not dared so far as to ask himself how he would save the hay after he had cut it. He cut it because the time had come to cut it. If he could not save it, he told himself in his self-pity and despair, he would let it rot where it lay.

He did not, he could not, ask his friends to help him. But they came. Before he could have asked, if he had been going to ask, they knew when he needed them, and they came. He asked himself accusingly if he had not after all depended on them to come, and he wavered upon the answer as on a cliff's edge.

They came bringing the tractor equipment they needed to rake and bale his hay. When they appeared, driving in after dinnertime on the right day, he was so abashed because of his debility and his dependence, because he had not asked them to come, because he now was different and the world was new and strange, that he hardly knew how to greet them or where to stand.

But his friends were not embarrassed. There was work to do, and they merely set about doing it. When Andy hesitated or blundered, Nathan or Danny told him where to get and what to do as if the place and the hay were theirs. It was work. It was only work. In doing it, in requiring his help in doing it, they moved him to the margin of his difficulty and his self-absorption. They made him one with them, by no acknowledgment at all, by not crediting at all his own sense that he had ever not been one with them.

When the hay was baled and in the loft and they had come to rest finally at the shady end of the barn, Andy said,

"I don't know how to thank you. I don't know how I can ever repay you." He sounded to himself as if he were rehearsing the speech to give later.

And then Nathan, who never wasted words, reached out and took hold of Andy's right forearm, that remnant of his own flesh that Andy himself could hardly bear to touch. Nathan gripped the hurt, the estranged, arm of his friend and kinsman as if it were the commonest, most familiar object around. He looked straight at Andy and gave a little laugh. He said, "Help *us*."

After that Andy again was one of them. He was better.

The great obstacle that remained was his estrangement of himself from Flora and their children. He knew that in relation to those who were dearest to him he had become crazy. He had become intricately, painfully, perhaps hopelessly crazy. He saw this clearly, he despised himself for it, and yet he could not prevail upon himself to become sane. He looked at Flora and Betty and Marcie as across a great distance. He saw them looking at him, worried about him, suffering his removal from them. He understood, he felt, their preciousness to him, and yet he could not right himself. He could not become or recover or resume himself, who had once so easily reached out and held them to himself. He could not endure the thought of their possible acceptance of him as he had become. It was as if their acceptance, their love for him, as a one-handed man, if he allowed it, would foreclose forever some remaining chance that his lost hand would return or grow back, or that he might awaken from himself as he had become to find himself as he had been. He was lost to himself, within himself.

And so in his craziness he drove them away, defending the hardened carapace of his self, for fear that they would break in and find him there, hurt and terribly, terribly in need—of them.

For a while, for too long, selfishness made him large. He became so large in his own mind in his selfish suffering that he could not see the world or his place in it. He saw only himself, all else as secondary to himself. In his suffering he isolated himself, and then he suffered his loneliness, and then he blamed chiefly Flora for his loneliness and her inability to reach him through it, and then he lashed out at her in his anger at her failure, and then he pitied her for his anger and suffered the guilt of it, and then he was more than ever estranged from her by his guilt. Eventually, inevitably, he saw how his selfishness had belittled him, and he was ashamed, and was more than ever alone in his shame. But in his shame and his loneliness, though he could not yet know it, he was better.

At that time his writings on agriculture had begun to make him known in other places. He had begun to accept invitations to speak at meetings that he had to travel to. On one of those wanderings far from home, and almost suddenly, he became able again to see past himself, beyond and around himself.

Memories of times and places he had forgotten came back to him, reached him at last as if they had been on their way for a long time. He realized how fully and permanently mere glances, touches, passing words, from all his life far back into childhood, had taken place in his heart. Memories gathered to him then, memories of his own, memories of memories told and re-told by his elders. The wealth of an intimate history, belonging equally to him and to his ancestral place, welled up in him as from a deep spring, as if from some knowledge the dead had spoken to him in his sleep.

A darkness fell upon him. He saw a vision in a dream. It was much the same as Hannah Coulter's vision of Heaven, as she would come to tell him of it in her old age: "Port William with all its loved ones come home alive." In his dream he saw the past and the future of Port William, of what Burley Coulter had called its membership, struggling through time to belong together, all gathered into a presence of itself that was far greater than itself. And he saw that this—in its utterly surprising greatness, utterly familiar— he had been given as a life. Within the abundance of the gift of it, he saw that he was small, almost nothing, almost lost, invisible to himself except as he had been visible to the others who had been with him. He had come into being out of the history and inheritance of love, love faltering and wayward and yet love, granted to him at birth, undeserved, but then called out of him by the membership of his life, apart from which he was nothing. His life was not his self. It was not his own.

He had become small enough at last to enter, to ask to enter, into Flora's and his children's forgiveness, which had been long prepared for him, as he knew, as he had known, if only he could ask. He came into their forgiveness as into the air and weather of life itself. Life-sized again, and welcome, he came back into his marriage to Flora and to their place, with relief amounting to joy.

He came back into the ordinariness of the workaday world and his workaday life, answering to needs that were lowly, unrelenting, and familiar. He came into patience such as he had never suspected that he was capable of. As he went about his daily work, his left hand slowly learned to serve as a right hand, the growth of its dexterity surprising him. His displeasure, at times his enmity, against his stump and his left hand slowly receded from him. They rejoined his body and his life. He became, containing his losses, healed, though never again would he be whole.

His left hand learned at first to print, in the fashion maybe of a first-grade boy. And then, with much practice, it mastered a longhand script that was legible enough and swift enough, and that he came to recognize as his own. His left hand learned, as his right hand once had known, to offer itself first to whatever his work required. It became agile and subtle and strong. He became proud of it. In his thoughts he praised its accomplishments, as he might have praised an exceptionally biddable horse or dog.

The prosthetic device also he learned to use as undeliberately almost as if it were flesh of his flesh. But he maintained a discomfort, at once reflexive and principled, with this mechanical extension of himself, as he maintained much the same discomfort with the increasing and equally inescapable dependence of the life of the country and his neighborhood upon mechanical devices.

And so the absence of his right hand has remained with him as a reminder. His most real hand, in a way, is the missing one, signifying to him not only his continuing need for ways and devices to splice out his right arm, but also his and his country's dependence upon the structure of industrial commodities and technologies that imposed itself upon, and contradicted in every way, the sustaining structures of the natural world and its human memberships. And so he is continually reminded of his incompleteness within himself, within the terms and demands of his time and its history, but also within the constraints and limits of his kind, his native imperfection as a human being, his failure to be as attentive, responsible, grateful, loving, and happy as he ought to be.

He has spent most of his life in opposing violence, waste, and destruction—or trying to, his opposition always fragmented and made painful by his complicity in what he opposes. He seems to himself to be "true," most authentically himself, only when he is sitting still, in one of the places in the woods or on a height of ground that invites him to come to rest, where he goes to sit, wait, and do nothing, oppose nothing, put words to no argument. He permits no commotion then by making none. By keeping still, by doing nothing, he allows the given world to be a gift.

Andy Catlett and Danny Branch are old now. They belong to the dwindling remnant who remember what the two of them have begun to call "Old Port William," the town as it was in the time before V-J Day, 1945, after which it has belonged ever less to itself, ever more to the machines and fortunes of the Industrial World. Now of an age when Old Port William might have taken up the propriety of naming them "Uncle Andy" and "Uncle Dan," they fear that they may be in fact the only two whose memories of that old time remain more vivid and influential than yesterday evening's television shows. They remember the company of Feltners, Coulters, Rowanberrys, Sowerses, Penns, Branches, and Catletts as they gathered in mutual need into their membership during the war years and the years following.

Andy and Danny are the last of a time gone. Perhaps, as they each secretly pray, they may be among the first of a time yet to come, when Port William will be renewed, again settled and flourishing. They anyhow are links between history and possibility, as they keep the old stories alive by telling them to their children and again, whenever reminded, to each other.

Sometimes, glad to be needed, they go to work with their children. Sometimes their children come to work with them, and they are glad to have help when they need it, as they increasingly do. But sometimes only the two old men work together, asking and needing no help but each other's, and this is their luxury and their leisure. When just the two of them are at work they are unbothered by any youthful need to hurry, or any younger person's idea of a better way. Their work is free then to be as slow, as finical, as perfectionistical as they want it to be.

And after so many years they know almost perfectly how to work together, the one-handed old man and the two-handed. They know as one what the next move needs to be. They are not swift, but they don't fumble. They don't waste time assling around, trying to make up their minds. They are never wrong about what is possible.

"Between us," says Danny Branch, "we've got three hands. Everybody needs at least three. Nobody ever needed more."

The Great Interruption: The Story of a Famous Story of Old Port William and How It Ceased to Be Told

(1935–1978)

Billy Gibbs was as lively a boy no doubt as he could have been made by a strong body, excellent health, an active mind, and an alert sense of humor much like that of his father, Grover Gibbs. Like about all the Port William boys of his time, his life was not as leisurely as he wished it to be. From the time he grew from the intelligence of a coon hound to that of a fairly biddable border collie, his parents, who were often in need of help, found work for him to do. This occasioned his next significant intellectual advance: recognition of the advantages of making himself hard to find. For the next several years, however, his parents, Beulah and Grover, were better at finding him than he was at hiding. From the time of their marriage in 1920 until Beulah inherited her parents' little farm in 1948, they were tenant farmers, and Billy was always under some pressure to earn his keep. Needing to work, for a boy of sound faculties, naturally increases the attractiveness of not working, and Billy's mind was perfectly sound.

His life would have been simple if he had been only lazy—or, as he himself might have said if he had thought to say it, only a lover of freedom. But along with the wish to avoid work, his mental development brought him also to the wish to be useful to his parents and to work well, especially if an adult dignity attached to the work. And so he was a two-minded boy.

And so he grew up into usefulness and a growing and lasting pride in being useful, but also into a more or less parallel love of adventure and a talent for shirking. Throughout his youth he remained, with approximate willingness, under the governance of his father, a man famously humorous and much smarter than he allowed his children to know. He managed Billy by demand, by challenge, and by pretending not to know what he knew he could not prevent.

If there were times when Grover kept Billy pretty steadily busy, there were also times when he did not. When Billy was not at work, he would be out of sight and free, as Grover expected and more or less intended. And so Billy got around. He hunted and fished and trapped mostly by himself, and with his friends he roamed about. There were few acres within a walk of his house that Billy had not put his foot on by the time he was twelve years old. His mind was free and alert in those days. He saw many things then that education and ambition would teach him to overlook. By the time he was fourteen he knew familiarly every aspect, prospect, and place in the neighborhood of Port William.

He knew, for example, that the Bird's Branch road curves down the hill past the old Levers place, where his family were tenants for many years, and goes on down and becomes fairly level and straight where the bottomland along the branch begins to widen and open into the river valley. In the summer of 1935, the year Billy would become fourteen at the end of September, an extremely brushy fencerow ran along the side of the road, and in this fencerow there was a gate, never shut, that led into a pasture abandoned just long enough to be covered with tall weeds and blackberry briars and so far just a scattering of seedling trees. If a gentleman from down at Hargrave wanted to conduct some business strictly private, he could turn his car through that gate, drive a hundred or so feet parallel to the *inside* of that fencerow, and become almost magically invisible to anybody driving a car or a team and wagon or even walking along the road on the outside.

He could be somewhat less invisible to a boy who would be across the road, fishing in the Blue Hole on Bird's Branch, would hear the car slow down, turn in at the gate, and presently stop.

Now who could have a reason to drive into that forsaken place in a car? And what might be the reason? And, to boot, in the middle of a Sunday afternoon. Billy of course wanted to know. He stuck the end of his fishing pole firmly into the ground and ventured across the road and through the gate. From there he could see the top of the car shining between the lowest leaves of the trees in the fencerow and the tops of the tallest weeds. He thought he could hear voices, perhaps a laugh, but a breeze was stirring the foliage and he was not sure. His feet were itching to creep up close enough to become informed. But the same itch made him cautious, even a little afraid. The business at hand, whatever it was, was strictly for grownups. And William Franklin Gibbs, among the several other things he was, was a mannerly boy, accustomed to granting respect, not invariably sincere, to grownups. The place, moreover, did not belong to him, nor he to it, a matter that concerned him only after he had become cautious. And he was enough of a hunter by then to know that he could not make his way secretly through the hard-stemmed weeds of the old pasture in broad daylight.

When he got back to the Blue Hole he saw from the bobbing and darting about of his cork that he had come into good fortune. Presently he drew out a nice sunfish, and for a good while after that his attention was entirely diverted from the mysterious car to the mysterious undersurface of the Blue Hole, where sunfish the size of his hand and bigger were expressing their approval of his worms. But when the car's engine started, quietly enough but loud enough to hear, of course he heard it.

This time he went no farther than the sort of hedge of leafy bushes and weeds along the roadside. As the car, a nice, new-looking blue car with a long hood, paused before pulling out onto the road, Billy could see the driver plainly through the windshield and then more plainly through the open side window. The man was important-looking, and intentionally so. He wore a dark jacket, white shirt and tie, a perfectly adjusted gray felt hat, eyeglasses, and a neat little mustache. Beside him but well away there was a lady, perhaps also important-looking, whom Billy could see even better. She too was well-dressed. She wore a nice little straw hat and a pair of dark-lensed glasses such as Billy had never seen worn by any woman he knew.

Billy did not then, nor did he ever, know who the woman was. But he instantly recognized the man as Mr. Forrest La Vere of the Hargrave upper crust, then running for public office. To make sure, as he really did not need to do, Billy waited until the car was well out of sight and then walked not many steps up the road to look at Mr. La Vere's picture on his campaign poster that was tacked to a big sycamore.

Billy Gibbs, who did not know what a cynic was, was not a cynic. But he had lived almost fourteen years within the farm life, social life, conversation, influence, and atmosphere of the Port William neighborhood, and he did not know when he had not known, and always a little more, of the ways of the world.

And so it happened, maybe as a mere coincidence but maybe not, that on the next Sunday afternoon he was again fishing in the Blue Hole. Again he heard the big, quiet car turn in at the open gate into the abandoned field, and this time he did not get up to look.

Or he did not go to look until the car had again spent its interval behind the bushy fencerow and driven away. And then, having again planted his fishing pole firmly in the earth of the creekbank, he followed the car's two tracks along the inside of the fencerow to the place where he could see that it had stopped before, and several times more than twice. He saw furthermore that just at the place where the car always stopped there was a stout tree, a box elder, that had grown leaning away from the fencerow into the open sunlight of the old pasture, as such trees do. It was a tree climbable enough, at least for Billy, who aspired to heights and was, if not yet avian as he would become in seven years, at least arboreal.

Toward the middle of the following Sunday afternoon, and certainly now by no coincidence, the young Mr. Gibbs—Billy Frank to his mother, of whom at the moment he was not thinking—was perched somewhat comfortably on a branch above the lowest branches of the box elder, which would position him, screened by the wider-spreading branch below, just about exactly over the roof of the big blue car. And when it came time for the car to arrive, here it came, and it stopped where it always had stopped before.

Mr. La Vere stepped out, took off his jacket, and placed it, neatly folded, on the hood of the car. He then went around and removed the back seat, placing it with some care on the ground and within the car's shadow. He and the lady sat down side by side upon it.

What followed Billy had seen enacted by cattle, horses, sheep, goats, hogs, dogs, housecats, chickens, turkeys, guineas, ducks, geese, pigeons, sparrows, and, by great good fortune he was sure, a pair of snakes. And so he was not surprised but only astonished to be confirmed in his suspicion that the same ceremony could be performed by humans.

And he certainly was getting his eyes full, except that the roof of the car was a little in the way, and there was yet a detail or two that he needed to study in case he might himself some day be called upon to assume the role of Mr. La Vere. He ooched therefore several more inches out along the limb and leaned ever so carefully a few more inches still farther out. And then he heard a crack that entirely distracted his attention from the drama below.

It was not a warning crack. The box elder being a brittle, humorless, unforgiving tree, the branch Billy was sitting on had no sooner cracked than it broke off near the trunk. Billy redoubled his hold on the branch above, which, with utter indifference to his great need and with a crack of its own, came loose in his hands, letting him down with some force upon the branch below, which, with the loudest and most eloquent of the three cracks, also broke and went down. To the Honorable Forrest La Vere, thus rudely interrupted in his devotion, it must have seemed that he had been assaulted by a flying brushpile, fully leafed and unwilted, with a boy inside it in a hurry to get out.

Billy came down perhaps a dozen feet in more or less the posture of an airborne flying squirrel, and landed squarely on top of Mr. La Vere. He lost no time in disentangling himself from the various limbs, and he was on his feet, running hard, no doubt before Mr. La Vere could complete the necessary change of mind.

But the force of Billy's descent had been considerably mitigated by the intervening small branches and foliage. The damage suffered by Mr. La Vere having thus been about entirely limited to his dignity and peace of mind, he too was very soon up and running. Although he had reached the far side of mid-life, Mr. La Vere was lean, evidently in good condition, well warmed up, clearly unresigned to second place, and his legs were longer by several inches than those of Billy Gibbs, who was after all still a growing boy.

Never before had Billy been obliged to think while running. But he thought then, surprised that he could do it, and he thought well. Like a hard-pressed rabbit, he had at first run for the nearest cover, heading up the hill toward the woods, but then, like a clever fox, he turned along the slope toward a thriving blackberry patch that had laid its tangles across the old pasture from one side to the other. This decision was costly to Billy, for without much damaging his clothes the barbed thorns, that snatched at his sleeves and pantlegs only momentarily, clawed long bloody scratches onto his skin, but they touched Mr. La Vere's imagination several seconds before he reached them. He was not dressed for briars. Taking care never to look back, Billy sped freely out of sight.

For three whole years, while Billy grew into wholehearted envy, not of Mr. La Vere's ladyfriend, but of his automobile, and while he watched the tops of young cedars and walnuts and wild plums and redbuds emerge from the weeds and briars of the abandoned field, he alone of all the people in Port William and the country round about knew the story which, after Wheeler Catlett came to know it, would be known as The Great Interruption. And likewise no doubt, of all in the urbs and suburbs of Hargrave, the only people who knew that story were the Honorable Forrest La Vere and the Unknown Lady.

The story must have lain on Billy Gibbs's mind with some weight, the more as he grew into the sophistication truly to appreciate it. He came to see it, or to imagine it, both as himself involved and as himself watching as from a higher limb. As it became more coherently a story in his mind, sometimes when he was at work alone he would tell it to himself, beginning with the leaning box elder and how he climbed it and took his seat, and he would laugh out loud, and would laugh more as he elaborated the details and again made them visible to himself.

One mind, and a boy's mind at that, finally could not contain such a story. But such a story, a story of such high excellence and so rare, could be turned loose in Port William only with some caution beforehand, as one might release an especially exuberant big dog. Billy found that he was not able to tell the story to anybody unworthy of it, which eliminated forthwith all the boys more or less of his own generation.

A part of the culture of Port William in those days was a curious division between the men and the boys. The men in their talk of sexual matters were fairly unguarded in the presence at least of the bigger boys. Their conversation did not as a rule *include* the bigger boys, but it went on without regard or respect to them, leaving them to understand what and as they could. And the boys never talked of what *they* knew in the presence of the men, though all of them knew the same things. Port William big boys and young men did not want to be caught presuming to be more grown up than they were. It would have been extremely irregular for a boy under twenty, or even twenty-five, to offer a sexual joke or a bit of sexual gossip to an older man. This was, in short, a boundary trespassed by the men regardlessly and often, but never by the boys except by accident, as when Orvie Galingale and Worth Berlew crawled under the hootchy-kootchy tent at the county fair to confront, not as expected the intimate revelations of the lady known as Bubbles, but their own fathers, who had paid already, as they thought, to get in.

Billy was balked also by the fastidiousness of a true critic. The boys he knew were just about uniformly no good as story-tellers, which suggested that they would not know a really good story from a pretty good one, and Billy knew he had a really good one. He wanted to tell it to a real story-teller who would recognize its worth. And so he told it to Burley Coulter.

Burley was a good friend and an old running mate of Billy's father. Burley and Grover Gibbs were not exactly like-minded, but they knew a lot of the same things, understood each other, and in essential ways depended on each other. And so Burley was in all but blood an uncle to Billy Gibbs. Since before Billy could remember, they had been on good terms. They trusted each other. And so if it should happen one winter night, as it did happen, that just the two of them, Burley Coulter and Billy Gibbs, should be coon hunting on the bluffs along Katy's Branch, that would be merely in the order of things.

As a coon hunter, Burley was easily pleased. If it was a good night for hunting and the dogs hunted well, he would be delighted to spend the necessary energy. If for whatever reason the hunting was poor, he would be about equally content to build a fire, sit staring at the blaze, and talk the unhurried talk possible at such times.

He and Billy had passed maybe an hour, now and again adding a stick or two to a fire large enough to give them its cheerful light and warmth but not too demanding of fuel. They had made the fire beside a large pile of rocks at the edge of a long overgrown tobacco patch. The ground was damp, and the rock pile offered a dry place to sit. They sat somewhat apart so as to face each other. Their talk had lapsed comfortably into silence and revived again two or three times, and finally Billy's silence was overpowered by the need to tell his story.

He said, "I'll tell you something." And then he said, "But now I don't want you to tell this to anybody else."

"Well," Burley said, "maybe I won't."

Billy in fact had not expected a better reply. If Burley had been another boy, Billy might have made him swear never to tell. But Burley was a man forty-three years old and Billy only a boy of seventeen. It may have been that Billy didn't mind much one way or the other. He was after all a two-minded boy.

Anyhow, he started into his story. Burley listened with what might have been respectful attention until Billy got to the part where he climbed into the box elder and took his seat on the second from the bottom limb and steadied himself by holding to the limb above, and then the big blue car followed its own tracks in from the road and stopped just where it had before, and then Mr. La Vere removed the back seat and situated it on the ground. And that was when Burley leaned back onto the rock pile with his fingers laced behind his head. "*Oh* good Lord!" he said, and started laughing.

If Billy told his story well, and he did tell it very well, that may have owed a good deal to the excellence of his audience. As Billy laid out the details just as he had done when he told the story to himself, and as the details accumulated, Burley's delight increased and he stopped laughing quietly only to laugh out loud.

When the story had been told, Burley sat up, thought a while, gazing into the fire, and from time to time laughed again to himself.

And then he said, "Well!"

In another little while he said, "Well, you knew the great man by face and name. Did he know you?"

"I never showed him my face. I had *some* sense."

"A little, I reckon. But you had as much as you needed, and you used it."

"Maybe I had even a little bit more than I used."

Burley ignored that. He said, "Hang on a minute. If I've figured this right, I'm now the fourth person in all creation that knows this story."

"Well, till I told you, I never told it, and I doubt if they ever did. Now don't you tell anybody else."

"You ain't got a thing to worry about. I ain't going to tell a soul but your daddy."

They both laughed then, for they knew equally that to tell Grover would be to tell Port William. He could have held such a story just about as long as he could hold his breath. And Billy was comfortable enough with that. He was too happy with Burley's pleasure in the story to want to deny it to others. He was a two-minded boy but purely and truly generous.

Billy never told the story again. He never needed to. It would be told from then on mainly by Grover and Burley. They were acknowledged story-tellers, long practiced, and as they told it they adhered to the outline of Billy's recital to Burley in the nighttime woods, but they added ever more artistry to the details.

"He done it, she done it, *they* done it," said Grover, who loved grammar mainly for its comedy. "They got entirely incorporated. Yes in-deedy."

"They never even shook hands," Burley said. "They got right into business with their hats on."

"*Aw* yeah," Grover said, "they went straight to the he-male and the shemale, conjugating that old verb to who'd a thought it."

"When that misfortunate lady heard them branches crack and saw that young brush pile coming down," Burley said, "her eyes popped out to where they looked at each other with some concern."

For a while after he told Burley and Burley told Grover, every time Billy heard the men laughing, he fairly reliably would know why. His story was again being brought to mind, either by being told or by being alluded to. For of course the story belonged richly and complexly to Port William, pertaining about equally to its geography and its history. It was a part of its self-knowledge. It meant in Port William what it could not mean, and far more than it could mean, in any other place on earth. The ones who told it and the ones who heard it knew the abandoned field and the brushy fencerow at the lower end of Bird's Branch. They knew the Blue Hole and the big briar patch. They knew Billy Gibbs, the boy he had been and was. They knew the nature and character of box elders. They had kept the stories of a greedy and miserly, eccentric and amusing family known around Port William as Leverses, who down at Hargrave were a family of greedy aristocrats know as La Veres. The tellers and hearers of the story understood in an ever-renewing instant the entire signification of their vision of the august Forrest La Vere conjugating the commonplace old verb upon an extracted back seat in a weed-field. Thus, for the men, the story was a way of knowing what they knew, and a way of teaching the boys. And of course the story made its way from the gathering places of the men into the kitchens and bedrooms round about and came to belong also to the Port William housewives and big girls.

From the night in the winter of 1938 when Billy set it free, his story was one of Port William's ways of knowing itself, but only for a few years. And then came the great tearing apart of the war and what followed. A new time came, different from any that had been before. Then, as the elders made their way one by one to their settled places in the graveyard, too many of the young became known to Port William mainly by their absence. Tom Coulter and Virgil Feltner and others perished in the war. The war promoted Billy Gibbs from tree-climbing to flying. He went into the air as a member of the crew of a B-17, and flew at last safely back to the ground with maybe a story or two he was not so eager to tell. And then he went to college, and from there, as his mother put it, "into a suit and into business." *That* was the defining story then, of Port William and thousands of places like it. It was the story of the young people, changed by the change of times, who by the war's end or the mid-century had found their way to city jobs and salaries or high wages, and who returned after that only to visit a bedside in a nursing home, at a loss for something to say, or to bury the dead.

I heard the story of The Great Interruption only a few

times in the years after the war. It was becoming less and less a property of its old community in time and place. Grover Gibbs and Burley Coulter, remarkably, had ceased to tell it. I think it had begun to make them sad. Port William by then was losing its own stories, which were being replaced by the entertainment industry, and so it was coming to know itself only as a "no-place" adrift in a country dismemoried and without landmarks.

Finally if Billy's old story were to be told, it would have to stand alone, bereft of the old knowing-in-common that once enriched it. It would be heard then as little more than a joke on the subject of what we have learned to call "sex," a biologic function dissociated from everything but itself. If one of the professionally successful descendants of the place as it once was were to tell it, say, at a cocktail party, it would be understood as an exhibit of the behavior of rural Kentuckians, laughable in all their ways, from which the teller had earned much credit by escaping.

Of the five children of Grover and Beulah Gibbs—Billy, Althie, Nance, Sissy, and Stanley—only Althie stayed close enough to accompany her parents and watch over them and share her life with them as long as they lived.

One day in the year or so between Burley's death and his own, Grover and I were sitting and talking on the tailgate of his old pickup truck. Grover had been kind to me ever since I was little. He was one of my own dwindling company of elders, and I loved to talk with him. We were talking, as we often did, of the changes that even I, younger than Grover by nearly forty years, had witnessed in Port William and the country around. We were telling of course the story, clearly ongoing and with no foreseeable end, of the departure of the people and the coming of the machines.

I said, "And the pore old ground is going to suffer for it."

Grover faced things by preference with a grin or a laugh that would be honest enough, for he had faithfully observed and relished the funniness of the world. But he could give you a straight look sometimes that made you shiver.

"Andy," he said. "Honey, I know you know. The hurts ain't all just only to the ground."

How It Went

(1979–1994–2002)

(1979)

This comes from Andy Catlett's memory of a day back when Pascal Sowers and the Rowanberry brothers, Arthur and Martin, were still alive, and they and all the younger ones still were strong. They were a neighborhood then, a company of kin and friends, none of whom ever worked at any hard task alone. In other times or on other days, various Coulters, Branches, and Penns might have been with them. Their heavy work in the barns or fields or woods brought together always their many hands, which lightened the work, and also their several minds from which they made, among their other necessities, much conversation, which also lightened the work.

They completed one another, not by proposing any such thing, as a marriage might, but merely by caring about one another and by being available when needed. From each of them Andy learned things good to know that he would not otherwise have known. When he lost his right hand to a corn picker in the fall of 1974, it was those others who made him whole in his changed life by conceding no difference to his loss, and by helping him, without his asking, when he needed help.

When they worked together, their work always rose above necessity. However hard or hot or uncomfortable it was, it was also a pleasure.

Not long ago, running into Pascal's son Tommy at town, Andy asked him a question he'd had on his mind:

"Tommy, what was the last year I helped you cut tobacco?"

"I don't know," Tommy said. "I can't tell you right off. But you know I miss them old times."

Andy misses them too, and his thoughts go back to them in wonder that such a settled companionship could ever have existed in the time past of a time present when Port William and its countryside are populated more and more by new-comers and strangers, mobile homes and modular homes. In the town, among the few old ones who are left, the question most often asked is "Who *was* that?" and the oftenest answer is "*I* don't know." Now in the onetime neighborhood of Port William neighbors may not even know one another, let alone gather their hands and minds together to lighten work.

———

HOW IT WENT

It was a morning in midsummer, already hot, and they were unloading hay into one of the small tin-sided sheds that Pascal had built in his pastures for handiness in feeding his cattle in the wintertime. Mart Rowanberry and Andy's boy, Marcie, who was then about seventeen, were handing the bales off the wagon. Art and Tommy and Andy were ricking the bales in the shed at the end where they had stopped the wagon, and Pascal, who was in a bad mood, was ricking at the other end by himself.

Nobody knew why Pascal was in a bad mood, but he plainly was. His mood plainly was one in which he did not want to get in anybody's way and did not want anybody to get in his way. And his mood was having an influence. Since they had begun the unloading nobody had said a word.

Their silence became socially awkward. Finally, perhaps to bring forth a resumption of good manners, Mart said, "Well, I reckon you all heard about that smart fellow down at Ellville can scratch his ass with his big toe."

The silence then resumed. It continued until Marcie, with the ostentation of patience by which a grown boy indulges his elders, said, "All right. I give up. How can that smart fellow at Ellville scratch his ass with his big toe?"

"Well," Mart said, "he got his thumb caught in some kind of a grinder. It was all mangled up to where they had to cut it off. And then they cut off his big toe and made him a thumb out of it."

Mart's explanation seemed to end the story. Nobody could think of another question. Nobody could think of another story that Mart's story reminded him of. Nobody spoke again. They went on unloading the wagon and building the rick in the shed, working then in the sort of approximate rhythm that establishes itself at such times.

Until, sounding unhappy that he could not forbear a comment, Pascal from his distance said, "He'd better be glad they didn't cut his *dick* off and make him a thumb out of it."

Nobody wanted to interfere with Pascal's bad mood. He had expressed one of the universal hopes of an age of medical miracles, but that was not all. He clearly had cast several aspersions, but nobody knew for sure which way they had flown or where they had lit. And so until that load was off nobody spoke again. But whenever any two of the rest of them looked at each other, there would be a grin, a look, or a snort, and already they were thinking carefully back over the details, preparing the story of that morning as they were going to tell it.

(1994)

Finally they dwindled until one hot, bright late August afternoon only four of them were at work in the tobacco harvest on the Sowers place: Pascal's wife, Sudie, who was the

Rowanberry brothers' much younger sister, Tommy Sowers's wife, Daphne, known as Daph, Tommy, and Andy. The Rowanberry brothers by then were dead, and Pascal had got too old to be capable of more than the piddling helps he occasionally offered.

They were housing a load of tobacco they had just brought in from the patch. The two women, turn about, were handing the sticks of tobacco—five stalks "speared" onto every four-foot stick—off the wagon to Andy. Andy, walking a long board between the wagon bed and an upended barrel, was handing the sticks up to Tommy. Tommy, who was standing in the tiers, was hanging the tobacco, the sticks and stalks of it carefully spaced, between the two tier poles at his feet and the two at shoulder height, where it would hang until it was cured. Pascal was seated on an upturned bucket against one of the posts along the driveway. From there he could watch both the work going on in the barn and, out the big open doorway, the vehicles that passed now and then along the road. He was not missing much. That year he was eighty years old and Andy was sixty, which made them, as they often noted, a hundred and forty years old. Tommy and Daph's granddaughter, Birdie, a pretty little girl two years old, for the moment entirely cooperative, was playing in the dust of the barn floor, variously talking and singing to herself.

The work of the four able-bodied grownups had been done by them and by others, dead and remembered, dead and forgotten, in years going back long before the coming of the tractor that had drawn the present load into the barn, and this year their work was carrying them through one of the last tobacco crops that would be grown on the Sower place. Though they did not yet know it, Pascal's last years would coincide with the last years of the tobacco program, which for sixty years had secured a measure of prosperity for farm couples such as Pascal and Sudie, Tommy and Daph. But for now, as if entranced by the old motions that they repeated over and over again, or like dancers carried by the familiar rhythm of an old song, they worked without speaking.

When this load was off, they would be on the downslope of the afternoon. They would pass the water jug then and gather round while Tommy would slice a water melon, as somebody in that family had done at that time of day in the tobacco harvest going back, at least to Sudie's grandfather, laying the green, white, and red slices, rind-side down, along the edge of the wagon bed for them to salt and eat. For perhaps half an hour then they would eat, rest, and talk, gathering strength and pleasure to ease them through to the day's end.

But the wagon was only half unloaded when the little girl quit her play and came running to the wagon, calling to her mother and making motions of urgency. She had something to say that needed to be whispered. Daph caught her lifted hands, swung her up onto the wagon, and leaned down to her. Birdie tiptoed and whispered.

"Oh," Daph said. "Good girl. Just go outside anywhere. It'll be all right."

Lifted down, Birdie ran not far beyond the doorway.

"Andy," Daph said. "Look."

And then they all looked as Birdie pushed down her shorts and, standing, peed a gracefully arching glistening stream, her own invention, of which she was proud.

There were laughs of appreciation and congratulation called out by the two women to Birdie, who was still in some need of such encouragement.

And Pascal, who still was sitting on his bucket, took off his hat, rubbed meditatively his bald head, and put his hat back on.

"Yeah," he said. "I used to go with an old gal could do that."

(2002)

There was nothing simple about Pascal Sowers. Like most farmers of his generation in that country, starting in childhood, he had done a lot of the hard handwork that, by commentators and experts who have never done it, is said to be "mind-numbing." But Pascal's mind, like that of many a farmer of his kind and time, was lively and capable. He was good at his work. He had studied closely a number of the people he knew or had known. He knew good stories and told them well.

Like the Rowanberrys, he spoke the language he was born to, that his parents were born to. Nothing he said, nothing in the way he spoke, had been learned from the radio or television. What does it mean, his friend Andy Catlett asks, when one speaks a language that is not public, that is shared and is so intended, but is not public? Partly it meant that Pascal lived a life entirely his own, not a life recommended by others, not a life advertised and sold.

In the presence of strangers or people with whom he was uncomfortable, he said little. He took himself seriously enough, and he did not wish to be taken lightly. If among his familiars he often said bluntly things that were astonishing or outrageous, that was partly to indulge and enjoy his aptitude for such eloquence. But partly also it was his way of brushing aside something serious that he had thought of and preferred not to say.

Or so Andy has come to think, after knowing Pascal for soon-to-be seventy years, and after thinking about him with particular tenderness and care since he and the others parted with Pascal, who finally was without a comment, at his grave on the hill at Port William.

The fact, anyhow, that Andy has had to keep returning to, circling about, and considering, is that Pascal was not an eagerly self-revealing man. If you wanted to know Pascal, beyond the often unignorable things he said or pointedly did not say, you needed to study carefully the originally swampy small river-bottom farm that he and Sudie bought in the forties, made over, carefully farmed, paid for, and modestly prospered on. To know his fairness and his gratitude you had to hear him in his bluntest way of speech giving credit, never to himself, but to Sudie for all he owed to her. To take the temperature of his heart, you had to notice his hospitality to stray cats and his attention to the personalities of dogs. His affection would be revealed by favors that he would do unexpectedly, disowning them as he did them, ignoring thanks.

One day when Andy came out of the bank in Port William and was crossing the road to his pickup, he was headed off by Pascal, who was carrying one of the devices known as "come-alongs," needful for lifting or pulling. It was a new one.

"You got a come-along?" Pascal asked.

"No," Andy said. "I don't."

"Well, you got one now," Pascal said. He pitched it into the back of Andy's truck and walked away while Andy was thanking him.

Maybe twice, at moments when it most counted, Pascal looked point-blank at Andy and called him "my friend." And this Andy cannot remember now without his eyesight blurring.

From his admirable competence at his work, which lasted well into his seventies, Pascal declined gradually down a long slope into uselessness. He suffered this with his customary disdain for falsification, and consequently with composure, even good humor. Anybody's attempt to overlook or be polite about his debility he cut off with a sentence absolutely declarative: "I am not worth a *damn*."

He foresaw clearly, and said, that he would end his days at Rest Haven down at Hargrave, for there would be nobody at home capable of helping him when he no longer could help himself. And when the time came he was taken, on his own advisement and demand, to Rest Haven.

Except for his "going down," as he put it, he stayed pretty much himself to the end, keeping his intelligent silences when there was nothing to be said, fending away overseriousness when necessary by his blunt declarations of the truth, bluntly serious when he needed to be.

One day when he visited Rest Haven, Andy had one of his granddaughters with him. Pascal was bedfast by then. When they entered his room he was lying straight and still with his eyes shut.

"Pascal?" Andy said, and Pascal opened his eyes.

"Why, I reckon so," Pascal said. "Come in."

"Pascal," Andy said, "do you remember this young lady? This is Flora, Betty's youngest girl."

And then Pascal seemed to gather his strength into his

eyes. He raised his head a little from the pillow and looked at Flora. She was a pretty girl. He studied her a moment with a kind pleasure he made no attempt to dissemble, and then he rested his head again upon the pillow.

"Ah," he said. "She's waiting for me, to be young."

The Branch Way of Doing

(1932–2004)

Danny Branch is older than Andy Catlett by about two years, which matter to them far less now than when they were young. They are growing old together with many of the same things in mind, many of the same memories. They often are at work together, just the two of them, taking a kind of solace and an ordinary happiness from their profound knowledge by now of each other's ways. They don't talk much. There is little to explain, they both are likely to know the same news, and Danny anyhow, unlike his father, rarely has anything extra to say.

Andy has always known Danny, but he knows that, to somebody who has not long known him, Danny might be something of a surprise. As if by nature, starting with the circumstances of his birth, as if by his birth he had been singled out and set aside, he has never been a conventional man. To Andy he has been not only a much-needed friend

but also, along with Lyda and their children, a subject of
enduring interest and of study.

Danny is the son of Kate Helen Branch and Burley
Coulter. His family situation was never formalized by a wed-
ding between his parents, who for various and changing reasons lived apart, but were otherwise as loving and faithful
until death as if bound by vows. And Danny was as freely
owned and acknowledged, and about as attentively cared for
and instructed, by Burley as by Kate Helen. "He's my boy,"
Burley would say to anybody who may have wondered. "He
was caught in my trap."

And so Danny grew up, learning by absorption the frugal, elaborate housekeeping of his mother through the Depression and afterward, and grew up also, from the time he
could walk, in the tracks of his father, which led to work, to
the woods, to the river, sometimes to town. Danny learned
as they went along what came from work, what came, more
freely, from the river and the woods, what came even from
the talk of his father and the other philosophers of the Port
William conversation.

The whole story of Burley Coulter will never be known,
let alone told. Maybe more than his son, he would have been
a surprise to somebody expecting the modern version of
Homo sapiens. He loved the talk and laughter of work crews
and Port William's loafing places, but he was known also

to disappear from such gatherings to go hunting or fishing alone, sometimes not to be seen by anybody for two or three days. Everybody knew, from testimony here and there, from gossip, that he had been by nature and almost from boyhood a ladies' man. Little girls had dreamed they would grow up and marry him, and evidently a good many bigger girls had had the same idea. But he remained a free man until, as he put it, Kate Helen had put a bit in his mouth and reined him up. But nobody had heard much more than that from Burley himself. He was full of stories, mostly funny, mostly at his own expense, but they never satisfied anybody's curiosity about his love life. He never spoke disrespectfully of a woman. He never spoke of intimacy with a woman. And so Port William speculated and imagined and labored over what it believed to be his story, receiving the testimony of many of its own authorities: "Why, he did! I know damn well he did!" And Burley quietly amused himself by offering no help at all. It is possible, Andy thinks, that Burley was the hero of a work of fiction, of which he was hardly innocent, but a work of fiction nevertheless, composed entirely in the conversation of Port William.

Burley knew the way questions followed him, and he enjoyed the chase, preserving himself unto himself sometimes, like a well-running red fox, by arts of evasion, sometimes by artful semi-truths. Those who thought to catch him were most apt to catch a glimpse as he fled or perhaps flew, a mere shadow on the horizon. When he stood and faced you, therefore, as he did stand and face the people he loved, his candor would be felt as a gift given. But in ordinary conversation with the loafers and bystanders of Port William, he could be elusive.

"Where was you at last night, Burley? I come over to see you, and you wasn't home."

"I stepped out a while."

"Well, I reckon your dogs must've stepped out too. I didn't see no dogs."

"My dogs do step out."

"Reckon you all was stepping out off up Katy's Branch somewhere?"

"A piece farther, I reckon."

"Well, now, where?"

"Well, till full day I didn't altogether exactly know."

"If I couldn't hunt and know where I was, damned if I wouldn't stay home."

"Oh, I knew where I was, but I didn't know where where I was was."

Danny, his father's son and heir in many ways, always has been a more domestic man, and a quieter one, than his father. In 1950, two years after the law allowed him to quit school and he started farming "full time" for himself, he married Lyda, and the two of them moved in with Burley, who had been living in the old house on the Coulter home place alone ever since his mother died.

For seven years Danny and Lyda had no children, and then in the following ten years they had seven: Will, Royal, Coulter, Fount, Reuben, and finally ("Finally!" Lyda said) the two girls, Rachel and Rosie. Lyda, who had been Lyda Royal, had grown up in a family of ten children, and she said that the Lord had put her in this world to have some more. Like Danny, she had grown up poor and frugal. "If my daddy shot a hawk that was killing our hens, we ate the hawk."

She was about as tall as Danny, stoutly framed but not fat, a woman of forthright strength and presence whose un-wavering countenance made it easy to remember that she was blue-eyed. She and Danny are the best-matched cou-ple, Andy thinks, that he has ever known. That they had picked each other out and become a couple when they were hardly more than children and married before they could vote seems to Andy nothing less than a wonder. He supposes that they must have had, both of them, the gift of precocious self-knowledge, which could have seemed only wondrous to Andy, whose own mind has come clear to him slowly and at the cost of much labor.

For a further wonder, Danny and Lyda seem to have un-derstood from the start that they would have to make a life together that would be determinedly marginal to the mod-ern world and its economy—a realization that only began to come to Andy with his and Flora's purchase of the Harford place when he was thirty. It was already present in Danny's mind at the age of sixteen, when nearly everybody around Port William was buying a tractor, and he stuck with his team of mules.

Marginality, conscious and deliberate, *principled* marginality, as Andy eventually realized, was an economic practice, informed by something like a moral code, and ultimately something like religion. No Branch of Danny's line ever spoke directly of morality or religion, but their practice, surely for complex reasons, was coherent enough that their ways were known in the Port William neighborhood and beyond by the name of Branch. "That's a Branch way of doing," people would say. Or by way of accusation: "You trying to be some kind of a Branch?"

To such judgments—never entirely condemnatory, but leaning rather to caution or doubt or bewilderment, for there was a lot of conventional advice that the Branches did not take—it became almost conventional to add, "They're a good-*looking* family of people." The good looks of Danny and Lyda when they were a young couple became legendary among those who remembered them as they were then. Their children were good-looking—"Of course!" people said—and moreover they looked pretty much alike. Danny and Lyda were a good cross.

Their economic life, anyhow, has been coherent enough to have kept the Branch family coherent. By 2004, Branch children and grandchildren are scattered through the Port William neighborhood, as Lyda says, like the sage in sausage. They stick together—whether for fear of Lyda, or because they like each other, or just because they are alike, is a question often asked but never settled. Wherever you find a Branch household you are going to find a lot of food being raised, first to eat and then to sell or give away, also a lot of free provender from the waters and the woods. You are going to find a team, at least one, of horses or mules. But there are Branches catering to the demand for heavy pulling horses. Some keep broodmares and sell anything from weanlings to broke farm teams. If a team will work cheaper or better than a tractor, a Branch will use a team. But with a few exceptions in the third generation, they also can fix anything mechanical, and so no Branch has ever owned a new car or truck or farm implement. Their habit is to find something that nobody else wants, or that everybody else has given up on, and then tow or haul it home, fix it, and use it.

As they live at the margin of the industrial economy, they live also at the margin of the land economy. They can't afford even moderately good land, can't even think of it. And so such farms as they have managed to own are small, no better than the steep-sided old Coulter place where Danny and Lyda have lived their married life, no better even than the much abused and neglected Riley Harford place that Andy and Flora Catlett bought in 1964.

The Branch family collectively is an asset to each of its households, and often to their neighbors as well. This may be the surest and the best of the reasons for their success, which is to say their persistence and their modest thriving. When the tobacco program failed, and with it the tobacco economy of the small farmers, and when, with that, the long tradition of work-swapping among neighbors, even acquaintance with neighbors, was petering out, the Branches continued to swap work. They helped each other. When they knew their neighbors needed help, they went and helped their neighbors. If you bought something the Branches had for sale, and they were always likely to have something to sell, or if you hired them, they expected of course to be paid. If, on the contrary, they went to help a neighbor in need, they considered their help a gift, and so they would accept no pay. These transactions would end with a bit of conversation almost invariable, almost a ritual:

"Well, what I owe you?"

"Aw, I'm liable to need help myself sometime."

The old neighborly ways of Port William, dying out rapidly at the start of the third millennium, have survived in Danny and Lyda Branch, and have been passed on to their children. The one boast that Andy ever heard from Danny was that he had worked on all his neighbor's farms and had never taken a cent of money in payment. After his boys grew big enough to work, and he knew of a neighbor in need of help, instead of going himself Danny would sometimes send a couple of the boys. He would tell them: "If they offer you dinner, you can eat, but don't you come back here with any money."

This uneasiness about money Andy recognizes from much else that he has known of the people of Port William and similar places. Free exchanges of work and other goods they managed easily, but transactions of money among neighbors nearly always involved an embarrassment that they had to alleviate by much delay, much conversation, as if to make the actual handing of cash or a check incidental to a social occasion. It was not, Andy thought, that they agreed with the scripture that "the love of money is the root of all evil," but that from a time even older they held a certain distrust against money itself, or the idea of it, as if a *token* of value were obviously inferior to, obviously worse than, a *thing* of value. And so a man, understanding himself as a neighbor, could not accept money as in any way representative of work or goods given in response to a need.

The Branches, then, would have things to sell. They would work now and then for wages. At convenience or if they had to, they would spend. But their aim, as often as possible, was to have a choice: something they could do or make or find instead of spending money, even of earning it.

Of the source and the reasons for this Branch fastidiousness, Andy is still unsure. For himself, he has finally understood that, however it may be loved for itself, money is only the means of purchasing something of real worth that is not money. To live almost entirely, or entirely, by purchase, as many modern people do, is to depress the worth of every actual thing to its price. And so the symbol limits and controls the thing it symbolizes, and like a rust or canker finally consumes it. Buying and selling for money is not simply a matter of numbers and accounting, it is also a dark and fearful mystery.

Do the Branches know this? Because he so imperfectly knows it himself, Andy has not known how to ask Danny or Lyda if they know it. He knows only that they, and their children too, seem to be living from some profound motive of good will, even of good cheer, that shows itself mainly in their practice of their kind of economy. The Branches are not much given to explaining.

And so in addition to being included in their friendship, benefiting from it, knowing them well, and loving them in just return, Andy has studied them with endless liking and fascination, feeling always that there is yet more that he needs to know. He believes that the way they live, and the way they are, can be summed up, not explained, by a set of economic principles, things Danny could have told his children but probably never did, never needed to. Andy, anyhow, after many years of observing and pondering, has made a list of instructions that he hears in Danny's voice, whether or not Danny can be supposed ever to have said them:

1 — Be happy with what you've got. Don't be always looking for something better.

2 — Don't buy anything you don't need.

3 — Don't buy what you ought to save. Don't buy what you ought to make.

4 — Unless you absolutely have got to do it, don't buy anything new.

5 — If somebody tries to sell you something to "save labor," look out. If you can work, then work.

6 — If other people want to buy a lot of new stuff and fill up the country with junk, *use* the junk.

7 — Some good things are cheap, even free. Use them first.

8 — Keep watch for what nobody wants.

9 — You might know, or find out, what it is to need help. So help people.

Andy heard Danny say only one thing of this kind, but what he said summed up all the rest.

When he was just old enough to have a driver's license,

Reuben, Danny and Lyda's youngest boy, raised a tobacco
crop and spent almost all he earned from it on a car. It was
a used car—Reuben, after all, was a Branch—but it was a
fancy car. Lyda thought the car was intended to appeal to a
certain girl. The girl, it turned out, was more impressed with
another boy's car, so Reuben got only his car for his money,
plus, as his mother told him soon enough, his good luck in
losing the girl. Though all in vain, the car was bright red, and
had orange and black flames painted on its sides, and had
a muffler whose mellow tone announced that Reuben was
more rank and ready than he actually was.

Andy and Danny were at work together in Andy's barn
when Reuben arrived in his new-to-him car. He had prom-
ised his help, and he was late. He drove right up to the barn
door, where his red and flaming vehicle could hardly have
looked more unexpected. He gunned the engine, let it gar-
gle to a stop, and got out. Maybe he had already had a second thought or two, for a touch of sheepishness was showing
through his pride. Danny favored his son with a smile that
Reuben was not able to look away from. Reuben had to stand
there, smiling back, while, still smiling, his father looked him
over. When Danny spoke he spoke in a tone of merriment—
the epithet he used seemed almost indulgent—but his tone
was nonetheless an emphasis upon a difference that he clearly
regarded as fundamental: Some people work hard for what

they have, and other people are glad to take it from them easily. What he said Andy has remembered ever since as a cry of freedom: "Sweetheart, I told you. And you're going to learn. Don't let the sons of bitches get ahold of your money."

The Art of Loading Brush

(2015)

I.

At last full of the knowledge of the wonder it is to be a man walking upon the earth, Andy Catlett is past eighty now, still at work in the fashion of a one-handed old man on what still he often calls in his thoughts the Riley Harford place, the name that has belonged to it for at least a hundred and fifty years. As a farm perhaps never better than marginal, the place in its time has known abuse, neglect, and then, in his own tenure and care, as he is proud to think, it has known also healing and health and ever-increasing beauty.

He has supposed, he has pretty well known, that some of his neighbors in Port William and the country around had thought, when he and Flora bought the place and settled in it, that they would not last there very long, for it was too inconvenient, too far from the midst of things, too *poor*. And so Andy has delighted a little in numbering, as disproof and as proof, the decades of their inhabitance: the 60s, the 70s, the 80s, the 90s. And now they have lived there more than half a century, long past the doubts and the doubters that they would last. Now it is beyond doubt or question their place, and they have become its people. They have given their lives into it, and it has given them a life such as they could have had in no other place.

Of all his kindred Andy has become the oldest. He is one of the last who remembers Old Port William, as he now calls it, as it was when it and the country around it were still intact, at one with its own memory and knowledge of itself, in the years before V-J Day and the industrializing of land and people that followed. He is one of the last of the still-living who was born directly into the influence of the best men of his grandfather Catlett's generation, who confidently, despite their struggles, assigned paramount value to the good-tending of their fields, to a good day's work with the fundamental handtools, to the stance and character of a good mule—the inheritance that, because he grew to welcome it, has made Andy so far out of place in the present world.

Surprised to find that he has grown as old as his grandfathers, who once seemed to him to have been old forever, he sometimes mistakes his shadow on the ground for that of Marcellus Catlett, his grandfather, whom he was born barely in time to know, or that of Wheeler Catlett, his father, whom he knew first as a man young in middle age and finally as a man incoherent and old. Their grandson and son, he has come at last into brotherhood with them.

Of all the old crew of friends and neighbors with whom he traded work and shared life, who accompanied him and eased his way, Andy is the last of the older ones still living. Of that about-gone association the only younger ones still at hand are his and Flora's children and Lyda and Danny Branch's.

Danny was the last, so far, to go. In the absence of the others, and not so often needed by the younger ones, he and Andy had been often at work together in their old age. "Piddling" they called it, for they never hurried and when they got tired they quit, but also it was work and they did it well. They had worked together since they were young. They knew what to expect from each other. They knew, as Danny said, where to *get*, and that was where they *got*. Danny knew, for instance, and maybe before Andy knew, when Andy was going to need a second hand. They worked sometimes, Andy thought, as a singular creature with one mind, three hands, and four legs.

Danny was sick a while. And then at breakfast time one morning, answering a somewhat deferential knocking on the front door, Andy was surprised to see Fount and Coulter Branch standing somewhat back from the door in the middle of the porch, formal and uncomfortable. They had never before in their lives come to his front door. Always all of them had followed the old usage: The familiars of a household went to the back door. But now the world had changed. It would have to be begun again. Fount and Coulter had come for that.

As Andy stood in the open door, the brothers looked at him and did not say anything—because, as Andy saw, they were not able to say anything.

And so he spoke for them. "Well, boys. Has he made it safe away?"

And then Fount cleared his throat, and swallowed, and cleared his throat again. "Andy, we was wondering, if maybe you wouldn't mind, if you wouldn't mind saying a few words for him."

They reached for his hand and shook it and went away.

And so Andy stood behind the lectern at the funeral home and spoke of Danny, of the history and company that they both had belonged to, of the work that they had done together, of the love that made them neighbors and friends, and of the rules of that love that they knew and obeyed so freely, that were so nearly inborn in them, as never to need to be spoken. Andy spoke the rules: "When your neighbor needs help, go help. When neighbors work together, nobody's done until everybody's done." Looking at the younger ones, his and Danny's, who now were looking back at him, he spoke the names of the old membership, dead and living, into whose company the younger ones had been born. He spoke of their enduring, their sweat, and their laughter. "This is your history," he said. "This is who you are, as long as you are here and willing. If you are willing, this is yours to inherit and carry on."

———

Having outlived so many and so much that will not be known again in this world, Andy has come to feel in body and mind sudden afflictions of sorrow for the loss of people, places, and times. He has passed the watershed in his life when he began losing old friends faster than he made new ones. Now he is far better acquainted in the graveyard on the hill at Port William than in the living town—than in the living country, in fact, and the rest of the world. And so he is diminished and so he lives on, his mind more and more enriched by the company of immortals who inhabit it. He is often given to the thought of subtraction, of what has been given, what taken, what remains. He is no longer surprised, when he is alone, to hear himself speak aloud a prayer of gratitude or blessing.

And yet by their absence his old companions have in a way come closer to him than they were when they were alive. They seem to involve themselves intimately in his life as he goes on living it. His thoughts now often seem to come to him in their words and voices.

On a certain kind of warm summer evening with a steady breeze from the west, Elton Penn will say to him again, as Elton said to him when he was a boy, "Do you feel how soft the air is? It's going to rain."

Or sometimes, when he is looking with satisfaction at

his steep pastures now healed and "haired over" with grass, he will hear his father say, "This land responds to good treatment."

Or when in the apparently unbreakable habit of the years of his strength Andy catches himself working too fast, Mart Rowanberry will say, as he said to him once with a certain condescension in the overeagerness of his youth: "You aiming to keep that up all day?"

Or he will remember sometimes in the evening, when the weariness of the day and of his years has come upon him, his grandpa Catlett speaking in one sentence the tragedy and triumph of his knowledge: "Ay God, I know what a man can do in a day."

Or he will hear again his granddaddy Feltner on occasions more than enough: "What can't be helped must be endured."

Or when, as sometimes happens, he is listening to somebody who has started talking and can't stop, he recalls the judgment of Art Rowanberry: "I reckon he must be a right smart fellow, but whatever he knows he learnt it from hisself."

As he thinks back over his kinships and friendships, of those he has loved and who have loved him, and of the once worn out and broken farm that he has cared for, that has responded to his care with health and beauty, he is able to think well enough of himself. But he still has his wits too, and his memory, and he is often enough reminded of his acts of thoughtlessness and selfishness, more in his youth than now, but also now, and he will hear his grandmother Feltner: "Listen to me. Your granny expects better of you." And so she taught him, as he flinched from her gaze, to expect better of himself. And so he is grateful to think of forgiveness and of the persons in high places who recommended it.

From Elton Penn's early death until the deaths as they came of all the older ones, Andy and his children, the Rowanberrys, the Sowerses, the Coulters, and the Branches would often be at work or at rest together. They knew one another well. They talked for hundreds of hours. And now it seems remarkable how little they spoke of public issues. They talked of course of the weather and their work, of things they remembered. They told jokes and stories. They told of other seasons in other years when they were doing what they were doing again. They told stories that all of them were in, that all of them already knew, that they had told and heard and laughed at and revised and told again any number of times. They told and wondered at bits of local gossip. They spoke of the life histories, commented upon the characters, and filled out the pedigrees of remarkable people they had known. Rarely they would lapse into journalism and tell of something they had read in the paper or heard on the news. Almost never did they speak of politics. Strengthened and sufficed maybe by the small events by which their world had lived, they spared one another the mention of the great events that were putting it to death.

Andy can remember now only one distinctly political utterance from a member of their old crew in all of those years. This was at one of the annual Rowanberry family re-unions. They had gathered that year in a hickory grove in a corner of a bottomland field belonging to Pascal and Sudie Rowanberry Sowers. There was a sizeable crowd of them: at-home Rowanberrys, Rowanberrys come home for the occa-sion, Rowanberrys-by-marriage, honorary Rowanberrys, and some self-appointed Rowanberrys who came bearing in pots, kettles, and baskets, as dutifully as the others, their contri-butions to the feast.

Andy was sitting on a bench among several of the men who had come from away, all of whom had originated within the familiar reach and compass of Port William, but who bore now something of the estrangement of distance and of other places. A little to Andy's surprise, they began to speak of the recent disgrace of an eminent politician. Pascal, who was standing with one shoulder propped against a tree more or less in front of the bench, seemed to be withdrawn under the brim of his hat as he could sometimes seem to be, but Andy knew that he was listening. The talk of the great poli-tician's downfall gradually brought one of the talkers under pressure to confess that he had voted for him, and another to say modestly that he had not.

Pascal then lifted his head so that his countenance emerged from the shadow of his hat. He said, "I'm not going to tell you who I voted for. But I'll tell you this much. I'll never vote for that son of a bitch again."

Ill-fitted as he has always been to the present age of the world, much more ill-fitted to it as he has come to be, Andy is yet in part and inextricably its creature, captured and held to it even by his contrariness against it, drawn too much left or right by the toxic simplifications of its politics, too much subject to the seductions of its economy. Often enough he knows he has spent money he knew he should have kept. Often enough he has been tempted to buy something he knew he did not need, only by a second thought separating himself from the dog-trained "consumers" who obediently pay too much for whatever is new. He knows that among that multitude he would disappear from the ghosts he most needs to remain known by. He rescues himself by vigilance and fear. And then invariably he will hear Danny Branch's admonition to Reuben, his temporarily youthful and extravagant son: "Sweetheart, I told you. And you're going to learn. Don't let the sons of bitches get ahold of your money."

Often enough in his remembering he will be delighted. He will laugh. And his laughter will be complicated by respect for the completeness and the stature that come only to the dead, and by the knowledge of loss, and by grief.

II.

Outliving your friends, hardly a pleasure, is in its way a matter not overly complicated. Time brings the losses and, if you stay in time, it removes the shock or surprise, gathers the new absences into the structures of ordinary days, and carries you past. But Andy also has begun to outlive his fences, and in the present age of the world that is a complication.

He had missed by a lifetime or more the age of the rock fences. When he was born some of them were still in use, but they were frost-heaved and crumbling. Nobody anymore had the skill or the time to mend them. They were being replaced by wire, the tumbled rocks left lying or cast into piles out of the way or knapped into road gravel. And so as he grew up he learned to fence with wire.

After he and Flora settled on the Harford place he renewed all the old fences and added more, sometimes with help but often alone. And then as the years passed he had repaired and then rebuilt the fences that he had built. But then he had been still in his strength, and for a long time when he needed help, he had his friends or his children to help him.

But now in his old age he still knows of course how to build a fence, but he is without the all-day strength and stamina to do it. And the generation of Port William men who knew either how to build a fence or how to help is by now as decrepit as he is or dead and gone. Of all the ones Andy knows the only one he could freely call on who could build a fence is Marcie, his son. But Marcie has his own farm and his own shortage of help. Though he is nearby and watchful and capable and always ready to help when needed, and often does help, Andy doesn't want to ask him to take on a big job. He feels a greater reluctance to call on any of the Branches. He knows that if he asked they would feel obligated and would come whether it suited them or not.

And so when he had spliced and re-tightened and stobbed up a lengthy stretch of old barbed wire to about its and his own limit, he started asking around for somebody else he could hire to rebuild it. A friend of his gave him the name of a friend of *his*, who gave him the name of Shad, short for Shadrock, Harbison.

Shad Harbison was an entrepreneur from down about Ellville who farmed some, carpentered some, did about anything anybody wanted done, including fence-building, and had a crew and the equipment to do the job. Andy called Mr. Harbison on the phone and told him what he needed. Would he be interested?

"Sure would," Mr. Harbison said. "I'll be there at eleven o'clock tomorrow morning. Now where you live?"

Andy told him, and told him how to find the place.

At eleven o'clock the next morning Mr. Harbison's pickup truck was in the driveway in front of Andy's house. Andy would not have been surprised if he had been late or had never showed up, but he was on time to the minute. Andy thanked him for his punctuality, and from then to the end of their association he would have no further reason to thank him. Mr. Harbison politely tooted his horn. They introduced themselves and shook hands.

Mr. Harbison, without unduly noticing the absence of Andy's right hand, had given him his own left hand. "Call me Shad."

"All right. And I'm Andy."

They walked the fence together, Andy showing Shad where it started and where it ended. Andy pointed to the old wood posts that were still sound, and to the ones that would have to be replaced. They took note of the considerable amount of brush and the several trees that would have to be removed before the old fence could be taken out and the new one built. They looked and Shad nodded at the half a dozen young oak and walnut trees that were not to be cut. Andy told Shad he wanted the bushes and the tree limbs laid in neat piles, butt ends together, handy to pick up. The old wire should be rolled up and the rolls put into piles. Andy described the fence he wanted: five strands of barbed wire, spaced so as to turn sheep. There was to be one new corner post, and Andy said how he wanted it braced.

Shad took it all in comprehendingly and with approval:

"Aw yeah. I see."

"Yessir, I see what you mean."

"Why sure. It won't be no problem."

They came to an understanding on the price. Too much, Andy thought, but he had expected that. He had made up his mind not to mind.

"Get the wire and everything else you need at Mel Hundley's in Port William. He'll know to look for you, and he'll charge me for what you get."

Shad then figured up and, taking a notebook and pencil from a shirt pocket, made a list of the materials he thought he would need. He read the list to Andy and looked at him.

"All right," Andy said.

And then, prompted by a committee of his ghosts, he said, looking Shad in the eye, "I'm asking you to do this because I think you'll do it right. I hate a damned mess, and I believe you do."

"Aw, I'm with you there. It ain't a *bit* more trouble to do it right than it is to do it wrong."

They shook hands.

"Tuesday week," said Shad. "Early."

"I'll be looking for you."

———

On Tuesday, not early, a large powerful red pickup truck with a large metal toolbox behind the cab came rumbling up the lane and into the driveway. The truck was pulling a large trailer of the kind known as a "lowboy" upon which was riding a large red tractor.

A large, soft-looking, somewhat sleepy young man got out of the cab and turned to look at Andy.

Andy was grinning to cover his displeasure at the looks of the young man. "If you're looking for Andy Catlett, I'm him." He stuck out his only hand.

Deciding what to do with it occupied the young man for an awkward moment, and then another, and then, turning his right hand approximately upside down, he allowed Andy to shake it.

"I'm Nub," the young man said.

"Are you Shad Harbison's son?"

"Well I *reckon*!" Nub said, implying that this should have been obvious.

By then an assortment of three other men had emerged from the cab. Had the surplus flesh of Nub been distributed evenly among them, they would have been much improved. They were lean with the leanness of wear and tear, of four or five Saturday nights a week for too many weeks. There was not a full set of teeth or a matched pair of eyes among them.

Andy put his hand in his pocket. "Fellows, I'm Andy Catlett."

"I'm Junior," said the first.

"I'm Junior," said the second, who clearly had looked forward to Andy's surprise at the coincidence.

"Twins!" Andy said, and the Juniors got a laugh out of that.

The third neither laughed nor smiled. He said, "Clay."

Andy turned back to Nub. "Where's your dad?"

"Bringing the wire and stuff."

They unloaded the tractor and Andy showed Nub where to leave the trailer. Then with Andy opening the gates and pointing the way, Nub driving the truck and Clay the tractor, they went up the hill to start work.

Andy had a prejudice against heavy machinery. When a big truck or tractor came onto his place, his prejudice was a sort of loose ache somewhere inside him or in the air around him. He had anticipated the truck and the tractor and was reconciled, but he had allowed himself to believe that they would be accompanied by a competent human.

When they had got to the fenceline and dismounted, he said to Nub, "I suppose your dad told you what we're doing here?"

"Well I *reckon!*"

But Shad, who was perhaps a competent human, still had not come. So far that was not necessarily a problem, for the line would have to be cleared and the old wire removed before the new materials would be needed.

Andy showed Nub everything he had shown his father. "Now you see what has to be done?"

"Well I *reckon*!"

By now Andy was conscientiously restraining his dislike for this slack-fleshed young man whose favorite three words bore invariably the whiff of condescension.

The two Juniors and Clay were unloading tools from the truck.

Andy had work of his own waiting on him that morning. He resolutely abandoned the fencing job to Nub and his crew and walked away. But he carried with him the insinuating small ache of his uneasiness, and his footing on the slope felt unsure, as if he were walking on mud.

When he went back, Shad had come with the supplies, which had been unloaded, and he and the crew were finishing their lunch in the shade of a tree midway of the fencerow. From there all the results of their morning's work were revealed to Andy. The brush, instead of piling it neatly as he had asked, they had merely flung out of their way. The old wire too they had rolled or wadded and flung out of the way. And they had removed not only the old barbed wire, but beyond that also perhaps two hundred feet of still very good woven wire they had so mangled in tearing it out that it could not be put back. Had Nub, the all-reckoning one, started the others and forgotten to tell them to stop? Had he been asleep? Was he perhaps awake only when at the wheel of his magnificent pickup truck?

After he had succeeded in believing his eyes, Andy turned to look at Shad, who was with perfect candor looking at him. Needing very much to say something, Andy thought of nothing.

It was Nub who first spoke. "It wasn't no sense in tearing out that good wire." His tone was corrective, even instructive, implying that the senselessness belonged to Andy, that *they* would never have thought of doing such a thing had they not been told to do so.

So far as Andy could think in the moment, and he was a slow thinker, he was licked. They had, however clumsily, taken him hostage. His old fence now was gone, he needed it, and they were the ones most available to replace it. Further thoughts, as he knew and feared, would come later. But when he replied his voice was quiet.

"No. There was no sense in it. Don't tear out any more."

He looked at Shad. "You're going to be with these people until they're finished, I hope."

"Aw yeah. I'll be here."

"And you remember how to space the strands?"

Shad recited the measurements, which encouraged Andy a little.

He said, "Well. All right."

He went back a few times to see what they were doing and to signify his distrust, but his judgment of them had turned hard and he went near them only by forcing himself. He was looking forward now only to being rid of them.

The full wherewithal of speech having returned to him, he was cursing them in his thoughts for their ignorance, idiocy, laziness, violence, and haste. He saw that wherever there had been a choice, they had preferred the easiest way to the right way. He was filled with an exasperation that he recognized as his father's: "Barely, by God, sense enough to swallow." He knew that he would not outlive their bad work. And he felt with a sickness almost physical their insult to his place, to himself, and to the history, the legacy, of the good work of his forebears and friends. He reminded himself that there had been a time when he had known hired hands, black and white, who had never possessed a square foot of their own land, who out of the common sense of their culture and upbringing would have recognized the badness of this work for what it was, and would have resented it.

But he had also begun an agenda of self-reproach that would be with him for a while. Why had he not fired Nub on general principles and on suspicion before he even started? Why had he not stayed with Nub and the others to watch, to supervise, at least until Shad had come? He began the suffering of self-knowledge.

He knew well his inclination to trust people, a weakness perhaps that he had nevertheless made a principle, for he knew, and upon enough evidence, that without trust there can be no end to the expense and effort of distrust. But now that it had been so flagrantly abused, his trust looked foolish to him. He looked foolish to himself. Those who had brought him up, whose ghosts accompanied him now, had told him plenty about caution, about responsibility, about the importance of "seeing to things" and "tending to business." And he had once in fact gone so far himself as to fire a man who had come to replace a barn door, and whose work was so careless and slovenly as to be destructive. The man apparently had concluded, as apparently Nub and Company had done, that a place so obviously inferior, so far off the road and out of the modern world as this old Harford place, did not deserve his respect or his best work.

But firing the man, Andy's one exploit as a firer, had given him no pleasure, not even in his initial anger, and the lapse of more than enough time had not taken away his distaste. But now, as he accused himself of not having fired or supervised Nub when he should have done so, it came to him that on the farms he had known in his early life he remembered nothing at all of supervising and firing. His grandfather Catlett, for example, had one hired hand: Dick Watson, a black man, whom as a child Andy had looked up to and loved, whom he still loves. Andy spent hundreds of hours in the company of Grandpa Catlett and Dick Watson. Though the order of work was set of course by Grandpa, he never in Andy's hearing told Dick *how* to do anything or made a supervisory remark. Past work himself, Grandpa would often be watching, but he spoke of Dick's work to Andy only to commend it, to speak of Dick as an example for Andy to learn from. "Look yonder at how old Dick sets up and takes hold of his mules."

Thinking back, Andy can see that Grandpa Catlett trusted Dick Watson to work well because Dick was capable of working well, did so willingly, took pride in doing so, and trusted Grandpa to see that this was so. They were, to the extent of their mutual trust, free of each other—free, that is, to sit down together on upturned buckets in the doorway of the barn to talk and look out at the rain. In that trust and freedom, limited as it was, there was something of peace, maybe even a promise of peace, unregarded and bypassed as history wore on through its wars into a time when no two men would sit together in a barn door to talk and watch the rain.

During his first twenty or so years, Andy played and then worked in the company of a good many hands, black and white, who worked by the day, straight time or temporarily as through a harvest. They and their work varied a good deal in quality, but with few exceptions, they were like Dick Watson far more than they were like Shad Harbison's fencing crew. Long ago the good ones, farm-raised and self-respecting, had either died or gone to jobs in industry. To replace them now were only the machines, the chemicals, and, in a pinch, the barely awake, the barely sober, the barely conscious, the incompetent, indifferent, and more or less accidently destructive.

At last, actually fairly soon, the Harbison crew messed and blundered its way to the completion of a passable fence, newer, shinier, and tighter at least than the old one. Andy wrote Shad a check for the too much that they had agreed on, that had now become much more than too much. Shad graciously accepted the check and hoped that Andy, if he ever had more fence to build, would just let him know.

"Thanks," Andy said, and watched their vehicles go down the lane and out of sight, he hoped, forever.

III.

And so he was left to submit his outrage to time, hoping, praying in fact, that before he died he would come to some manner of forgiveness both for Shad Harbison's crew and for himself.

Unignorably in the way of that lay the mess that the fencers had left behind: the scatters and tangles of brush and small logs, the randomly discarded rolls and wads and bits and pieces of old wire that now defaced and affronted the beautiful field that for fifty years he had housekept. There had been a time when in his strength he would have thought nothing of cleaning it up. He could have done it by himself in a few hours. Now he was depressed and diminished by it. It looked impossible.

He thought of calling his son to come and help him, but he rejected that thought as soon as it came. It was too late now to ask Marcie. If he had asked when he should have, the two of them working together would have built a good fence with no mess or shortcutting. Moreover, they would have enjoyed working together.

Now, grieved by that loss and dismayed by the result, he was also embarrassed. He could not bear the thought that Marcie might *see* the mess. He knew Marcie would not say, but he dreaded that he would think: "Well. You oughtn't have dealt with those damned counterfeits in the first place."

Andy knew very well why he had dealt with them: He was ignorant and knew it and was in a hurry and went ahead anyhow. And so he didn't call Marcie.

But there was one recourse he might still have. There was a good boy from down at Hargrave, Austin Page, a boy not farm-raised but interested in farming, who had asked to work for Andy while he was in high school, and Andy often had been glad to hire him, to have his help, and to have his company. He *liked* Austin, who was intelligent, eager to learn, willing to work, and humorous enough to put up with the correction he sometimes received. Andy had put him to the test a number of times, and Austin had always passed. By way of Andy's instruction, and sometimes his impatience, Austin had learned to work *with* Andy. Now more often than not he knew where to get, and more often than not he could anticipate what came next. Now he was in college, majoring in music, in which he was perhaps exceptionally gifted. As Andy had grown older and weaker, Austin had grown older and stronger. He was a big boy now, well-muscled, with freckles and tightly curled hair the color of a new penny. He was easily embarrassed and a radiant blusher, which made him especially valuable to Andy.

"I can turn that boy on and off like a light bulb," he said to Daisy Page, Austin's mother. Daisy Page was a woman whom Andy somewhat excessively admired, and all the more when she replied, "Mister. Catlett. You are too near the dropoff to be a smartass."

She said that as a prelude to saying that Austin soon would be done with his summer courses and was wondering: Might Andy have work for him before he had to return for the fall semester? Andy said yes, he might.

And so it happened that about three days after the departure of Harbison and crew, when Andy was sorely needing him, Austin called him up.

"Mr. Catlett, this is Austin. Do you need some help?"

"Do you mean am I helpless?"

"Oh nosir. I mean, do you have something to do that I could help you with?"

"Yes, Mr. Austin, my friend, I do. Come in the morning."

Andy had a small, low-wheeled wagon that was easy to load. It was not often used, and he and Austin had to go to some trouble to get it out from among the other implements where it had been put away. When they had it unencumbered and in the clear, they brought out Andy's old team of horses, the white one and the black, and hitched them to the wagon. By then Andy felt that he too had come into the clear. The oppression of the fencers and their mess had lifted from him like a cloud.

In his new clarity he had a sort of vision of himself and Austin there with the team and wagon at the start of their morning's work: an old man full of an outdated pride and demand, counting his losses, still suffering his dream, two nights ago, of the handtools of all the tradesmen of Old Port William heaped up and auctioned off to "collectors" who did not know their uses—and, standing beside him, this vivid boy, his mind on fire, his hair burning his cap off, this Austin Page, fresh from his summer courses, clearly glad now to be with Andy, outdoors, going to work.

Andy handed the lines to Austin and was amused, also much pleased, that Austin took them as a matter of course into his own hands and spoke to the team.

They went up to the fencerow. When they had come to their starting place Andy said "Whoa," and he and Austin stepped off the wagon.

Andy said, "You see what we've got to do. It's a mess."

And Austin, quoting and correcting, said, "A damned mess," and Andy laughed.

"We'll pick up the brush first," he said, "and we'll pile up the wire as we find it. It's scattered everywhere. We'll pick that up last. Finding all of it'll be the problem." In fact they would not find it all that day. As Andy expected, he would be finding the smaller pieces by surprise for a long time. Once, as he had feared, he found a fugitive hank of the heaviest of it by cutting into it with his mowing machine.

He picked up the first limb and laid it on the wagon. And then Austin picked up a somewhat larger one and, from a distance of perhaps a dozen feet, with a young athlete's depreciating nonchalance, tossed it over onto the one Andy had loaded.

"Hold on!" Andy said. "Wait a minute." He had spoken almost before he thought.

In his happiness at Austin's arrival to help him, Andy had seemed to himself to be both in the moment and outside it, watching. And now, his mind as if alerted in all the strata of its years, he was inhabiting also a moment much older. He was fourteen years old and had been formally hired, not at last by his father but by Elton Penn, to help in the tobacco harvest, and thus, small for his age as he was, had arrived at last at the status and dignity of a hand. But he had just handed Elton a stick of tobacco, turning loose his end as soon as Elton took hold of the other and greatly increasing the effort for Elton.

"Now *wait* a minute!" Elton had a transfixing grin, and Andy was transfixed, knowing well by then that his situation could get worse.

"You handed that stick to me *wrong*. Now I'm handing it to you *right*. Now you hand it back to me *right*. That's the way. That's the way I want you to hand it to me from now on."

Andy said, "Austin, my good boy, damn it, wait a minute. We ain't going to make a mess to clean up a mess. Do you want to put one load into three loads or into one load?"

He looked at Austin until Austin said, "Well. Obviously. I would rather put one load into one load."

Andy saw that Austin's ears were turning red, and he was amused, but he said fairly sternly, "Well, come and pick up that branch you just threw on and turn it over so it takes up less room. Now snug the butt up against the headboard of the wagon.

"That's right," he said. "That's the way we do it. We pick up every piece and look at it and put it on the load in the place where it belongs. We think of the shape of every limb and stem and chunk and pole, and that's the way we shape the load.

"It's the use of the mind," he said, "what they ought to be teaching you in school."

Andy and Henry, his brother, had gone to see Elton one day maybe two years after Old Jack Beechum had died and Elton had bought the Beechum place. In Old Jack's declining years he had been for a while dependent on hired hands, each of whom had left a deposit of things unwanted, things put down and forgotten. Now Elton had torn down the small house built for hired help and was setting the place to rights. The Catlett brothers found nobody at home that day, but in the barn lot there was a wagon loaded with trash, unusable scraps of old lumber, and the rocks that Elton had picked up here and there. Henry stopped the car and he and Andy sat for a few minutes, admiring the load, which was, of its kind, a masterwork. Every piece, every scrap conferred upon the whole load the happiness of its right placement.

"He couldn't make an ugly job of work to save his life," Henry said.

"*Now* you're shouting," Andy said to Austin. "Now you're doing it right.

"Now," he said, "we're practicing the art of loading brush. It is a fundamental art. An indispensible art. Now I know about your 'fine arts,' your music and literature and all that—I've been to school too—and I'm telling you they're *optional*. The art of loading brush is not optional."

"You talking about symphonies?" Austin had stopped and was standing still to signify the importance, to him, of symphonies.

"Symphonies! Hell yes!" Andy said. "You take a society of people who can write symphonies and conduct symphonies and play symphonies and can't put on a decent load of brush, they're going to be shit out of luck."

Austin's face, starting with his ears, had become almost astonishingly red, and Andy rejoiced. He was bearing joyfully now the burden of knowing better. Maybe in the passing on of his ghostly knowledge he was doing his duty to Austin. He was sure that a man hiring a boy had a duty to help him along if he could. But his thoughts were moved now by a parental fear for this Austin, this boy with his mind on fire, kindled by symphonies and God knows what. Andy was entirely familiar with that fire. Any sorry poor human having a mind, some time or another it would be on fire, with the old prospect of burning the mind's owner or burning the world, invoking always the old familial hope, for every grown boy anyhow, that the heat might be so contained as to warm a hearth or boil a kettle without burning down the house. So an old man, leaning toward a young one, would try to dampen a little the omnivorous blaze. But also he would be warming his hands. He felt a strange elation coming into his heart, so familiar now among the dead, so strange among the living. He wasn't going to say much more, but for the moment he was standing his ground.

"My dear Austin, my good boy, maybe it's possible to blow things up and burn things up and tear things down and throw things away and make music all at the same time. Some, it looks like, think you can. But: If you don't have people, a lot of people, whose hands can make order of *whatever* they pick up, you're going to be shit out of luck. And in my opinion, if the art of loading brush dies out, the art of making music finally will die out too. You tell your professors, when you go back, that you met an old provincial man, a leftover, who told you: No high culture without low culture, and when low culture is the scarcest *it* is the highest. Tell 'em that. And then tell me what they say."

Now instead of blushing Austin was thinking. His face, his posture, his movements all now bore the implication of thought.

He said finally, "I reckon you'd make brush-loading a required course for music majors."

Andy laughed, which he had been wanting to do for some time. "I probably would, if it was up to me. But listen, Austin. I'm serious."

"I know it."

"And I'm telling you all this because I'm your friend."

"I know it."

———

They finished the load. Andy took the lines himself this time. He stood to drive, and Austin made himself an uncomfortable place to perch.

"The art of *piling* brush begins and ends," Andy said, "with knowing where to pile it."

He drove some distance to where a grassy slope came down to a wooded bluff. They came to a swale in the pasture where once there had been a gulley, now long-healed and sodded over, "haired over" his father would say. But the gulley was still open and raw where it steepened, going into the woods. Andy positioned the wagon just above that place.

He had a theory, two hundred years too late to prove, that gullies like this one had been opened by plowing and cropping the slopes. Before that, when the country still wore its deep, porous, rootbound original soil, the water draining through such places was more apt to seep than to flow. Where the slopes were not too steep they could be healed under grass. On the bluffs, even after the trees had returned, the healing would be slow, if it could happen, if it could happen in human time. Andy nonetheless loved the thought of the healing of the gullies. He knew they could not be healed from the bottom up, for there the flow had gathered too much force. But for a good while he had thought, experimentally, that by using brush to slow and divert the water a little just below the edge of the grass, he might start the healing from the top. He laid his thinking out for Austin, showed him what he had in mind, and then to the head of the gulley they applied the art of piling brush.

And so they worked through the morning. And so they worked to the end of their task in the middle of the afternoon. By then Andy was tired. By then Austin was doing most of the work, and all of the hardest of it. Andy was keeping out of his way, helping a little as he could, and watching, as Austin stepped with the happiness of his young strength into the work. About as far as it could be done in Andy's lifetime, they had undone the bad work of the fencers. Maybe they had helped a little the healing of the hurt world. And he was proud of the boy.

A Time and Times and the Dividing of Time

(1944–2019)

I.

In the afternoon of a gray Friday in February 1944, Andy Catlett rode the school bus from the Hargrave school to its place of turning around on the Bird's Branch road near Port William. From there it was a walk of half a mile or so to the house of his Catlett grandparents on the farm that his family called "the home place." He was not one of the bus's regular passengers. It could carry him only as far as the end of its established route. This day and this trip would begin one of the dominant patterns of his early life: his passages back and forth between his parents' household in Hargrave and that of his Catlett grandparents on the home place, between town and country, that from then on would give him a disruptive sense of his own oddity.

The memory of that afternoon, when he stepped out of the confinement of the bus and its enveloping sound and smell into the felt breadth and chill of the open country, has stayed with him for three-quarters of a century. Except for the foreclosure of nature and his numbered days, it might last him as long again. He would then have been just about nine and a half years old, a count he would have been keeping, for he longed to be ten and to write his age in two numbers. And that pretty well exhausted his use, so far, for arithmetic.

With the increase of physical idleness in his old age, he has acquired almost the ability to see himself as he was then: a boy small for his age and in his own estimate and foreboding forever too skinny, carrying his book satchel into which, over his objection, his mother had inserted a neatly folded extra shirt and his toothbrush. Better than he can see himself as he was, he can see as he then saw the segment of his native country that lay before him as he began his walk: its winter-silenced hollows and ridges, its bare trees, the lichened and moss-grown rock fence then still standing alongside the two-track gravel road. Behind him he could hear, for he disdained to look, the yellow school bus turning around and heading back, empty, to Hargrave.

As he walked he was watching the world, which seemed to turn backward under his feet as he stepped along, and in his mind he was saying after the manner of writing in books, "The boy has got off of the bus. He is walking on the Bird's Branch road toward the home place."

He had not been at the home place with his feet on the ground under his own guidance since the new year had begun. After so long an interval in town and school, the life of schedules and ruled streets, and his out-of-school life with his fellow boys, he felt a strangeness about himself, and about the place, that would take him a while to get over. The change that would be coming slowly to him was that out there in the country, in the big unbounded air with not a building yet in sight, life was not shaped just by other people's expectations, but by seasons, days, and weathers, and by work done when it was time to do it.

Though he could not have said so at the age of nine and a half, he felt that he was walking from one time, one kind of time, into another, and he was somewhere between them. As if watching from the air, at a remove of seventy-five years, old Andy feels the modern age, the "post-war world," in the offing, and he is grateful for the little while of his childhood when he was still innocent of it. If the departing school bus is an intrusion of the future of schooling and the time to come, the boy Andy is now walking step by step back into the old time, the time before, so far hardly enough intruded upon to trouble its ignorance of the future.

Andy felt somewhat rebuked by his knowledge of the home place and the older, longer time that adhered to it, as if fearing a little that he looked schoolish or still carried with him, trailing in the air behind him, the smell of school. But with all the country around him, stepping alone upon the surface of it, hearing only the sound of his own footsteps on the packed gravel, the awareness grew upon him that he was intact and free. It occurred to him that at that moment only he in all the world knew where he was. The thought was new to him and vast, for he had never before been by himself so far out of sight and sound of all other people.

He gave no more thought to his family down at Hargrave than he gave to his teacher and his schoolmates. He was happy to be where he was, and he missed none of them. If it had been summer, and he was out like this somewhere among the farms, he would likely have been with his uncle Andrew. And so as he went along, Uncle Andrew came to his mind, and he did think for a while of Uncle Andrew, for as always when he was not with him he missed him. Being with Uncle Andrew was fairly often an adventure. As old Andy knows with familiar sorrow, looking back, Uncle Andrew was a man often at large, an unruly and a reckless man. If it was a summer day and Andy was with Uncle Andrew, the two of them might be at work at something somewhere for a while, or they would stop by where Jake Branch and his crew or the Brightleafs were at work to see if something might be needed to help them. And then they might drop back down to Hargrave to the Farm Supply Company to get a replacement part and to talk a while, or to stop by the Triple A office to talk with the ladies there. Or, if it was a day when Uncle Andrew was extra thirsty, they would stop by Slope Sims's store to get a soft drink and talk a while with Slope, who probably would be lying on a countertop cushioned by a litter of bills, receipts, old sacks and wrappers, and dried onion skins, with his feet drawn up and his head propped on his hand, smiling as he listened and talked. Wherever they went, Uncle Andrew was welcomed by his friends, and they would talk and laugh. Their hilarity, for it was often that, rode upon references to matters of the world of grownups that to the young Andy were mysterious and utterly interesting. He would imagine himself as a grown man leaning with his elbow on the counter at the Triple A, filling his pipe, and saying casually something that would make the pretty women laugh. The other grownups Andy knew did not make such references. At times he would be aware, and this made him proud and troubled, that as his uncle Andrew's bosom friend, he knew him as he was not known to the family's other grownups. He knew that Uncle Andrew would say anything whatsoever that he thought of. And old Andy knows that Uncle Andrew was likely also to *do* anything whatsoever that he thought of.

His knowledge of Uncle Andrew so filled Andy's mind that he had to stop and stand still a while just to think. The problem of course was that, even so far, Uncle Andrew required more thought than Andy was capable of thinking. And capable of thought as he might become, he will not have finished thinking about his uncle in seventy-five years. Andy was named for Uncle Andrew. Sometimes when he had to sign his name in school, he would write "Andrew Catlett, Jr."

Andy got the uneasy feeling sometimes that his parents

might not know everything about Uncle Andrew that maybe they ought to know, but so far as he could tell they loved Uncle Andrew and were at peace with him. But when he and Uncle Andrew would eat their dinner with Grandma and Grandpa Catlett, as they often did, the air could get full of some trouble that Andy would not understand. Grandma sometimes would be worrying and fretting over Uncle Andrew more than she worried and fretted over Andy, wanting him to eat some more of this or that, or drink another glass of buttermilk. And a couple of times when Uncle Andrew had to jump up from the table and rush out the back door in the midst of dinner, Grandma would shake her head and say to Andy in a tone of great sorrow, "Oh, that poor boy has always had such a delicate stomach."

Andy may not have known that Uncle Andrew was forty-nine years old, but he knew he was not a boy. When Grandma spoke of him as "that poor boy," something was wrong.

Except when they would be making a joke about Andy's appetite or praising his future, Uncle Andrew and Grandpa never had much to say to each other, and Andy knew that there was yet another misfit of some kind. If Andy was staying at the home place, and he rode past Grandpa on his pony without having his mind on his business, Grandpa would say, "Sit up! Take hold of her! Damn it, you ride like your Uncle Andrew."

Though he had spent maybe his share of time in Grandpa Catlett's lap, he was aware of a difference, an unlikeness that was almost a distance between Grandpa and himself, also between Grandpa and everybody else. More than anybody Andy would ever know, Grandpa belonged to the unconditional world, its weather and its work. Far more than he belonged to the house, he belonged to the barn and the fields. He belonged to his saddle mare, Rose, who served him as his sons already were served by automobiles. He belonged to the living, willing strength of teams of work mules. If internal combustion had disappeared overnight entirely from the world, Grandpa might not have noticed. As Andy finally has come to think, his grandpa had most characterized himself when, in his final summer, he would get up as always at four o'clock, eat his breakfast, go to the barn, sit down on an upturned bucket, and go back to sleep. If he had remained in charge of himself, he would have died in the barn. Though as a boy Andy felt his grandpa regarding him with a fierce and fearful love and from a distance, he was nevertheless absorbing an influence and gathering memories that would instruct and shape him for the rest of his life.

During much of his childhood, Andy would sometimes go into what his mother called a trance, which was one of her several reasons for wondering what was going to become of him. If she had seen him standing there in the road, slack-mouthed and unseeing, she would have said, no doubt

correctly, that he was in a trance. His thoughts had gone off
and left him as empty of himself as a young scarecrow. What
put him back together again was his book satchel that he
needed to shift into his other hand, the chill that was coming
through his clothes, and hunger. He knew he was expected.
His grandmother would have begun to listen for his footfall
on the boards of the back porch. The big meal at her house
was dinner. She wouldn't be fixing a lot of supper, but she
knew he was coming, and she would have something for him
that he especially liked.

Consciousness and purpose having returned to him, he
began to hurry. The thought came to him that by now his
friend Dick Watson might be at the woodpile, splitting wood
for Grandma Catlett's kitchen stove, and so he hurried a little
faster. He wanted to get there in time to help Dick carry in
the split wood to fill the woodbox. Though Dick was a black
man becoming elderly and Andy a young white boy, they then
were, as far as Andy was concerned, the two halves of a settled friendship. Having pondered that old alliance through
all the intervening years, Andy has acquired a certain courtesy by which he submits to question his childhood's simple
faith that they were equal in their affection for each other.
The question is courteous because he allows it to remain forever unanswered. But he is fairly assured that Dick often had
been glad of his company, and he thinks he may have loved
Dick Watson then more perfectly than he loved anybody else,

for he always minded Dick and was never contrary with him. Because of Dick's seniority, Andy knew that he was expected to defer to him and mind him, but that requirement was so exactly balanced by Andy's willing deference and obedience that it might as well not have existed. During the several years allowed to their friendship, old Andy thinks it never occurred to him that it was possible for him to disagree with Dick or to disobey him. Though Dick sometimes had to admonish Andy, and sternly enough, mainly in the interest of keeping him alive, it was never for impudence or disobedience. Of all his elders, moreover, Dick was the one Andy was most eager to help at work, and so to learn Dick's way of working. Unlike Uncle Andrew, Dick really worked—when there was work to do, he kept at it steadily until it was done or until quitting time—and so helping Dick, when he knew he was really helping, gave Andy the worth and dignity that he longed for.

And so he hurried. When he got in sight of the house and barns and other buildings at the home place, he stopped a minute to listen, and sure enough he heard the sound of Dick's axe at the woodpile. He ran a while then before he walked again, really hurrying. To old Andy it seems that he very nearly sees the boy he was, stepping fast along the road, even as he thinks again his old thoughts, and sees again through his young eyes the country lying around and the road ahead.

And now Andy Catlett, at the age of eighty-four and a half, having recovered so vividly the memory of himself at the age of nine and a half, begins to watch over his young self as a helpless bystander. Old sorrows, undiminished however time and thought have worn them, begin to make their way again into his heart. For the boy, who is walking as if backward in time to the home place that is still for a while intact and intelligible in the old ways of the time of Grandpa Catlett, is walking also into the time to come.

What the old man knows but the boy does not is that, within two years of that day, three of the main supports of the life that had shaped him so far and forever, and so far also had sheltered him, would have departed from this world: Uncle Andrew, Dick Watson, Grandpa Catlett. In old Andy's mind the three names resound over the hollows and hills of retrospect like strokes of a tolling bell, unheard yet in the silence that surrounds the unsuspecting small boy who was himself. And his informed heart hurts with his wish to reach out his hand.

II.

"Andy, remember now to pay some kindness to your grandma. She loves you and will want a share of your company. Don't just light there and run off like a let-loose young barn cat."

That was Wheeler Catlett, Andy's father, thinking as usual of things that Andy ought to do and was apt to forget.

Andy would not have thought of that himself, for he was not practiced in dutifulness, let alone sympathy and self-correction. But he was glad for a change to be told to do something he did not mind doing.

When, having slept like Grandpa in his underwear and shirt, he came down to breakfast the next morning, and panicked a little at seeing only his own place at the table still set, he knew that his grandma had let him oversleep, had probably forbidden his grandpa to wake him up.

"Where's Grandpa?"

"Out," she said, and from her tone he guessed that some opinions had been exchanged about her inclination to spoil him. "Out," she said. "Somewhere in the *beyond*."

And so she named to Andy exactly where he wanted to go. But he sat down at his place, and she began in her emphatic way to prepare his breakfast. Presently she set before him a plate warm from the stove, furnished with scrambled eggs, sausage, and two buttered hot biscuits. With the same emphasis and intent she filled his glass with milk and plunked down a jar of blackberry jam with a spoon in it.

"Eat! Eat it up while it's hot!"

She hovered over him, urging him to eat and to eat more. It was not that he had no appetite. He could eat so much, as she sometimes said, that it made him poor to carry it. And she did not want him to be fat, but only to be big. To be bigger. To have the protection of bulk against the diseases that might afflict him. She feared for him. He was too small and skinny for his age. Sometimes she seemed to have come to him on a mission from the local history of plagues—diphtheria, typhoid, cholera, smallpox, scarlet fever, flu—to warn him and do all she could to protect him.

"Eat!" she said, buttering another hot biscuit and putting it on his plate as she might have thrust a stick of wood into the stove. "There's not enough of you! You'd have to stand twice in the same place to make a shadow!"

But he ate, with what she called "a coming appetite," a large breakfast, to her satisfaction, and to her despair that it would not do him enough good.

When he had finished, his wish to go straight to the barn was strong enough to remind him not to do it. Once he had canceled that wish, he was happy, as he often had been before, to keep company with his grandmother. It was perfectly agreeable to him to tell her, in answer to her questions, as little as possible of his family news and with appropriate selection and some improvement, of his life in and out of school.

So they talked while she washed the dishes and he dried them, and while, with such help from him as she would allow, she made the beds and subdued dust and disorder in the front rooms. As they worked, making little noise and talking quietly all the while, Andy began to hear also the house's silence. Old Andy, in whose memory and mind seventy-five years later the old woman and the boy go about their day, still hears that silence, old and long, that contained the speaking and then the ceasing of many voices.

In that silence, after her morning chores were done and they had sat down by the kitchen stove to rest before she would be starting dinner, Grandma resumed her musing on the past, which now in her old age was always near to her. As it seemed, and seems yet to her grandson, she remembered everything that had troubled her life, from the greatest so far of her griefs to various lamented broken dishes and how they had got broken. She remembered also many things that had pleased or amused her, but ever in her mind was the foreshadow of loss and sorrow. She knew, she never forgot, that whatever she had lost was lost forever. She felt the vulnerability of all flesh to any catastrophe she could imagine. As her grandson, clarified by the gathering of his own years, would eventually know, and this sealed forever his loyalty to her, his grandma was not a happy woman. Maybe there was some quality or degree of happiness that had never come to her, and would never come. He remembers forever finding her in the darkened upstairs bedroom that they seldom used, lying on the old iron bed, struck down by what was now forever too late to prevent. "Oh honey, we'll never see your uncle Andrew again. We never will see him anymore." She did not sound like herself then or for a long while afterward. They lived on, their lives for a while seeming to rattle loosely in so large an absence.

In addition to her own, Grandma had memories yet older that came to her from her mother-in-law, Elizabeth Coulter Catlett. Grandma called her "Miss Lizzie" and served her pretty much as a daughter in that house during the first twenty or so years of her marriage. Perhaps because she never knew her own mother, Grandma listened to Miss Lizzie, and would remember her, with a deference that she granted afterward to nobody.

In so many years while the old woman talked and the young one—Grandma! but younger than Andy as a boy could imagine—listened, the older memory was delivered into the younger one. When Grandma in turn delivered it as breath and light into the memory and imagination of her young grandson, and when he in his turn had grown old, a long time in his home country seemed to have happened also in his own memory, and to him.

His grandmother's tellings might not have sunk into him so permanently had he heard them in a different house. But that house, with the old silence that he heard in it, with the look and feel of long wear in its lived-in rooms, seemed to him to verify the stories told in it. Two of its rooms, the dining room and the parlor, were set apart, their furniture once but no longer offering itself as nice. Formally announcing an aspiration, that the rest of the house did not pretend even to remember, to visitors who rarely came, those rooms mostly were kept shut. The rest of the house—kitchen and living room, the bedrooms upstairs—to the boy Andy was utterly familiar and comforting, and so it remains in memory to Andy grown old. But old Andy sees in them everywhere what he now knows to be the marks of money trouble, of self-denial and making do: the several coats of cracked and blistered paint on the table and chairs in the kitchen, the remnants of sets of dishes and silverware that his grandma mourned over as her "nice things," and in the other rooms the more or less accidental assortment of mismatched furniture, some pieces long-kept and prized, others there merely for being needed, and over it all the unifying stains and shines of wear. As he recovers these things in his thoughts, so late in his life, thinking of their hard times with debt and low prices and each other, there will come over Andy a longing to lean over the old man and the old woman, his grandparents, and gather them like children into his arms.

In his childhood the old house was both a present comfort and the setting for events that belonged to it a century and more ago. As she told her memories of memories, his grandma spoke as a witness, as if seeing what she was telling. To the boy it was merely knowledge, which his grandma made sure he learned, that the house had once been home to Elizabeth Coulter Catlett and her husband, Mason Catlett—Grandmother and Grandfather, as they required their grandchildren to call them, and as they are called still by Andy's grandchildren. But the stories about them in his grandma's telling came into Andy's mind with breath and being, as things seen, not in full clarity—the faces never came into focus—but as visions, even so, partial or blurred, but never changing from their first appearing to him.

He sees Grandmother sitting on the step to the back porch of the house as he knew it. She is hulling peas. As she works, a man whose satchel identifies him to her as a traveling salesman leaves his horse and buggy and, seeing her, starts toward the house. She allows him to approach, but before he can offer his greeting, she looks up from her work. "We've all got smallpox here."

The salesman somewhat rapidly begins backing away, explaining, apologizing, begging her pardon. Just as Grandfather appears, coming perhaps from the barn, the salesman backs into a large stump and falls backward over the top of it. Grandfather says, "There now, Lizzie. You've talked him to death."

They were members of the supervisory, not to say meddlesome, Bird's Branch Baptist Church, within which they did not very comfortably fit. But considering the times in which they came of age, married, and started their family, they seem to have been remarkably and perhaps carefully unpolitical. They owned slaves—not many, for their farm was not large—but as the sectional difference grew into the Civil

War, they did not lean to either side. Grandfather was thirty-eight years old in 1861, young enough to have been a soldier if either side had attracted his devotion, and he was the son of a soldier of the Revolution. They certainly were not Yankees or Unionists, but also not Confederates. Maybe they were among the forlorn adherents of Kentucky neutrality.

Their devotion went certainly to each other, their children, and their farm, which they struggled to hold onto. Their attitude toward it maybe can be assessed from the character of Andy's grandpa, who in his turn carried forward both the devotion and the struggle. Their attitude toward slavery maybe can be assessed from the little that has been remembered of it.

One day when Grandmother was taking an after-dinner nap by an upstairs window, she heard the slave woman Violet tell the cat, "Old Lizzie's asleep, and I'm going to beat the hell out of you."

"Old Lizzie," who would then have been in her thirties, told that to her daughter-in-law with an amusement that clearly cherished Violet's spunk, which to Andy suggests a certain indulgence, a certain amity. But what, after knowing the story for a lifetime, is he to conclude from Violet's announcement to the cat?

He remembers also, from his grandma's telling, that at the onset of a solar eclipse Miss Lizzie saddled her horse and rode in the dwindled light to find the hands where they were at work, for she knew they would be afraid. Andy came eventually to recognize a measure of sympathy in that, but he does not know how to weigh it against the violence and heartbreak that he knows were implicit in the ownership of humans by humans. What he very clearly does know is that when she went directly to the barn and saddled her horse, his great-grandmother was entirely in character. She would not have waited for somebody to do for her what she could do for herself.

Andy reflexively thinks of her as "the old woman," then having to remind himself that at the start of the Civil War, she was thirty-four years old, and his grandpa would not be born for three years. As a girl, she planted a lilac bush that was still living and blooming when Andy was a boy. That is all the knowledge of her young life that has come to him. In her early years she must have had an independence of mind and character that stayed with her into her marriage, for as wife and mother she had when she needed it a readiness to decide and act, answering to nobody, that Andy would know in his father. Whether it was only by her resolve or by Grandfather's also, they appear to have had no intention regarding the Civil War, except to keep out of it.

And so Grandfather's military experience cannot have lasted much more than an hour. In the summer of 1864, when Grandpa Catlett was, as he said, "a little bit of a baby laying yonder in the bed," soldiers, mounted men, came in the night, captured his father, ordered him to mount behind the saddle of one of them, and rode away with him. For whatever reason, maybe she was occupied with the baby, Grandmother did not confront the soldiers at the house. She understood what had happened only as they were riding away. But without a pause even to pick up a garment, she set out behind them, wearing only her nightgown. They easily outdistanced her, of course, but she knew where they were camped on the next ridge. To Andy it has always seemed that he can see her as she followed the road, then barely a road, down into the hollow and up the hill: a tall woman, lean like his grandpa and his father and himself, just visible in the darkness, walking fast, one hand lifting the hem of her long gown safely above the dust.

She had somewhat the power of startlement as she stepped in her nightgown into the firelight of that camp, where the soldiers by then had unsaddled their horses. She had the power also of the large dignity of her anger, and of her will that did not regard or hear what they were saying to her. She reached for Grandfather's hand and led him back into the dark and on home.

On another night another small band of soldiers came, not this time to kidnap a recruit, but on speculation. They made so free of the house as to find and carry away "a very fine gun," as Andy's grandma put it, that had been given to Grandmother by "a gentleman who admired her." However it may have happened, it was again the lady of the house who followed them to their camp and, by the exercise of the same powers, took back her weapon. But then—and here Grandma reproduced Miss Lizzie's amusement at herself— she realized that the soldier who had taken her gun had loaded it. She was afraid to fire it and afraid to carry it home loaded. And so she handed it back to the thief, ordered him to fire it, and he did.

Where were the men? Where, when the gun was taken, was Grandfather? Why was it Grandmother who had to go out in defense against armed men? It took Andy a long time to know enough and think enough to realize that if the things she did had not been done by a woman they could not have been done. She alone had had the character and confidence to act in the spaces offered to her by her time's deference to women, spaces the more available to her because so few women of her time trespassed into them.

If Andy ever knew which side those soldiers belonged to, he has forgotten. It may be that his grandma had forgotten. Probably it does not matter, for by then the war remaining in Kentucky had been reduced to a general disorder, in which nighttime acts of violence might be committed anywhere by any of a number of sides for any reason. Since apparently they were in uniform, the soldiers could have belonged to the Union army of occupation or to some roving band of Confederates or to the county's Unionist Home Guard. In Grandma Catlett's mind, the hearsay of those years of war was so darkened that the boy Andy would be surprised when it finally came to him that his people had lived then partly in daylight and by days of more or less ordinary work.

III.

The story that held them longest, that they returned to most often, that has kept Andy in wonderment all his life, as perhaps his grandma in all of hers, was the story of a girl named Molly Webb, which happened also to be another story of Andy's formidable great-grandmother, Miss Lizzie.

Molly Webb must have been a pretty girl, as it would have been hard not to think, and no doubt a good girl, in her young life happy enough. And as Grandma knew for sure, this girl was in love with Samuel Wheeler, a boy who in fact was Grandma's much older first cousin, the son of her father's brother James. And then as the war fell upon the country, it came as a great sorrow to Molly Webb, for the boy Samuel made himself a man by joining a unit of Confederate cavalry that was recruiting in the neighborhood, and by doing so in defiance of his father's settled allegiance and most stern admonition.

But the girl Molly was twice misfortunate, for after her lover was gone past coming back any time soon, and then was gone forever, and therefore as he would never know, "She found herself to be with child," Grandma said, "nature being what it is, and God help us."

And so Molly Webb joined her story to the story of the war, and in only a few months passed from a girl's love and desire to a widow's sorrow and a woman's travail. But she passed also, and as quickly, into a sort of exile, for as soon as her pregnancy become unconcealable, her rigidly godly parents disowned her. "Turned her out!" Grandma said. And Molly was henceforth as dead to them because of her sexual offense as she was, because of that and because of Samuel's political offense, to his father.

"After that," Grandma said, "the *pore thing* found somebody to let her work for room and board. But that couldn't last. Of course." And looking somewhat piercingly at Andy, she said, "Maybe you had better remember. When a baby is on its way into this world, it don't wait for its circumstances to improve.

"That girl," Grandma said, "was in the fix of stray dog, about to give birth to a stray pup. What could she hope for, turned out that way, where people were poor and torn apart and afraid? All the foothold she had on this earth was nothing but just her life, and her baby's."

So there was Molly Webb in her relentless predicament that Grandma knew or remembered only in its bare outline. But as her term was fulfilled and the birth of her baby close upon her, she grew desperate for somebody—"somebody," Grandma said, "in all the wide world"—to stand up for her, her never-made marriage, and her child. And so she set out

in the early dark of a winter night, on foot, alone, telling nobody. "Without a word to a living soul," Grandma said. "And
just think how far in trouble she was!

"But you don't know," Grandma said, looking hard at
Andy. "You're a long way from knowing. And a long time. It'll
be some other girl's good fortune, some day, if you can get
capable of knowing."

It was Elizabeth Catlett—"Miss Lizzie" to Grandma, to
Andy "Grandmother"—who saved Molly Webb. Grandma
told this story as all of a piece, as no doubt it existed in her
mind by the time Andy was there to hear it. For a long time he
knew it as she told it, as he knew by memory and reminding
the story of his growing up. It was only after he had learned
to test the order of causes and effects and the sequences of
events that he realized how much of his grandmother's story
of Molly Webb he—and even perhaps his grandmother—had
never known. They did not know, of course, those things that
only Molly Webb herself could have known. In his childish
bewilderment at things he had begun to suspect, Andy had
wanted to know about the courtship of Molly and Samuel.
How long were they sweethearts before Samuel rode away?
"God knows," Grandma said with an emphasis that acknowledged the great and fearful difference between God's knowledge and hers.

But there were questions more practical and necessary to
the completion of the story. Where and with whom did Molly

live between the discovery of her pregnancy and the birth of her baby? If she slipped away on that fateful night without telling anybody, as apparently she did, how was her absence discovered? And how did Grandmother, Miss Lizzie, learn of her disappearance? And how, once she knew the girl had disappeared, did she know where to find her?

The last of those questions, within limits, can be answered. Given what she might well have known, and probably knew, and what she could imagine, she would have known where to look.

As Grandmother imagined, Molly had followed the main road to where it dipped into the swale below the Bird's Branch church. She left the road there and walked back a long lane, between a rail fence and the bank of the creek, to the log house of Samuel Wheeler's then widowed father—whose neck, Grandma said, "was so stiff with Unionism and righteousness that he couldn't turn his *turr'ble* old head."

The girl knocked, the door opened, was held while the light of a carried candle fell upon her, and then, decisively, was shut. So much, of course, she later told.

But where on that night was Grandfather? Grandmother at that time had young children. Her oldest child, a son, born in 1850, would have been capable, for a while, of looking after his little sisters. Or maybe the slave woman Violet was then living in the room over the kitchen. But why was there no man of either race available, or whom she would have trusted, to do what she herself did? And Andy finally concluded that what she did had again required a woman to do it. She, after all, was almost certainly the one who knew where to look. The questions anyhow were answered on that night as completely as they needed to be.

As she did at other times, she stepped simply and directly into the duty that came next. She would have lighted a lantern of the sort, so Andy has imagined, still carried at night by farmers and hunters until he himself was a grown man. She went to the barn and harnessed the nearly white mule they called Old Tom and hitched him to the sled.

The lantern, once she started the mule, would have been no help. Maybe the night was clear, starlit or moonlit. She would have depended on her knowledge of the way and on the old mule's utterly reliable disdain for suspectable footing. She drove to the swale below the church and turned onto the narrow shelf of the lane to the James Wheeler place. And she found Samuel Wheeler's unwedded widow, the unclaimed Molly Webb, her baby already born, lying in the poor shelter of a rail fence corner beside the lane along the creek, and she brought them home.

So long afterward, Andy can see the boy he was, sitting still far longer than he had ever sat still in school, listening to his grandmother speaking into the still room the memory of a woman forty years older. No more than Andy had his grandma lived and moved and had being in that past and gone darkness and the just-sufficient light that had shone in it. But Miss Lizzie, who no doubt had afterward needed to imagine it for herself, had given it over into Grandma's imagination, and Grandma had given it into Andy's.

As it happened, Andy knew from the early years of his own life how to harness and hitch a mule. And he knew, he could see, how it would have been to do so at night and in a hurry by the light only of a lantern. As he sees himself listening to the story of that night, he sees also how the lantern and the sky would have lighted the whiteness of the mule. He can hear the sled runners grating over the rocks and sliding quietly over the dead leaves. And he hears the small outcry, startling in the cold dark, of a human being new to the air and reduced to the life striving to live within it and the love surviving in its mother's hands.

In his latter years, remembering memories of memories twice his age and yet his own, Andy has thought again and again of that night and of that time. He can recover readily enough, with the increase in his old age of his freedom to ponder, the simplicity, the simple openness, of his young mind as he listened to his grandmother. But the books he has read, along with the growth of his experience and his thoughts, through all the years that have followed, though enlarging his knowledge of the Civil War, have rendered it imaginable to him only in other bits and fragments. It is whole to him now only as a great waste of life and suffering and a burden to be borne. He thinks of the unforeseeing rhetoric of the politicians, of the weariness and the dusty roads, of the muddy roads and the mired wheels, the horse and mule teams overladen and exhausted, of the outcries of defiance and of suffering in the riddled air, of the flesh-littered fields and the buzzards circling. Out of all that, compounded day by day for four years, would come great, perhaps everlasting, results to be weighed and debated by learned scholars perhaps forever. But also this: Two women and a newborn child, drawn by a worthy old white mule, making their way to shelter, in the dead of night in the dead of winter.

"But then what happened?" Andy asked more than once, and he still would like to know. "What ever happened to Molly Webb? What happened to the baby?"

"Honey, I don't know. I don't know if I ever knew."

Aside from their mutual home country and her carved name and dates in the Port William graveyard, the only material relic of his great-grandmother that Andy possesses is a copy of a portrait photograph sent to him by a cousin in Mississippi, another of her great-grandchildren. At the time of the photograph she was elderly. By then, to her neighbors a generation younger, she was "Aunt Lizzie." A widow for maybe fifteen years, she is wearing a rather elegant black dress, chastely ornamented, with a high collar and at her throat a broach with a large dark stone. Her still abundant white hair is beautifully parted and swept back. Her face is unlined and finely made. There is, Andy thinks, a considering gentleness in it, but also much of strength. Behind the wire-rimmed small lenses of her spectacles, her eyes, without asking or offering, look straight out of the picture. Her mouth was by then made straight by suffering and endurance, the lips pressed firmly together, and yet it is a comely mouth that would freely laugh. When he looks at her picture now, he is reminded both of her gift for comedy and of the two small graves beside her own on the hill at Port William—graves that, when they were new, she sent Grandfather to cover with boards to protect them from the rain.

To look at her as she presented herself to the photographer, as no doubt to have looked at her on the day before or the day after one of her forcible interventions, you would have thought her perhaps a remarkable, perhaps a remarkably self-possessed, but not an extraordinary housewife of her time. What the old woman, so conventionally self-respecting in her photograph, actually had within her of character and capability may be suggested by another photograph given to Andy by his cousin. In that picture one of her daughters and one of her granddaughters are sitting one above the other on a flight of steps going up to the entrance of a town house, probably in St. Louis. The daughter was delightedly remembered by Andy's father as "Aunt Suzy." The granddaughter, of about his father's age, Andy himself remembers from the times in his childhood when she would come from St. Louis to stay a few nights at the home place. He called her "Cousin Rose." The two of them, the older in her fifties, the younger in her twenties, are sitting as if it has never occurred to them to lean back. They are somewhat alike in their faces, but much more alike, Andy thinks, in bearing and demeanor. They have about equally in their eyes, as they look at the camera, a challenge of some kind. Both are smiling, but not as women ordinarily smile for a camera. They smile as if they are not very earnestly suppressing laughter. They have the look of two smart women who enjoy knowing several things that they are not going to tell.

They were storied women, both of them, who occupied distinctive places in the memories of Andy's grandma and his father, and so in his. It was known, for instance, that Aunt Suzy could not resist her sense of the ridiculous. One day she was alone on a train, wearing, for a reason never explained, a red wig. A gentleman took the seat beside her and began to make himself pleasing, as he thought, by complimenting especially her beautiful red hair. She encouraged him by thanking him most graciously and in turn complimenting his manners. By the time the train arrived at the gentleman's station, the two of them had become cordially acquainted and hoped to meet again. When the gentleman stepped onto the platform and turned to bid farewell to Aunt Suzy, she replied by leaning out the window and waving her wig.

Cousin Rose, to her own delight in the telling, had committed something of a disaster by agreeing to chauffeur a family member's car, which she did not know how to drive, assuming that if anybody else could drive a car, then of course she could. But she also traveled alone to India to study theosophy, a word that Grandma Catlett pronounced tastingly as if it were an exotic food, but also with respect for Cousin Rose. Grandma did not explain theosophy to Andy, and Andy did not ask her to do so. He thought it an interesting word because of its strangeness. In the way of a boy who trusted some adults, he thought it probably had a meaning somewhere above his comprehension.

Pondering those photographs, remembering his memories, thinking his thoughts, after all, Andy thinks that the woman known as "Miss Lizzie," later as "Aunt Lizzie," as "Grandmother" to his father and to him, must have been what horsemen sometimes call "a grand matron." For surely she had passed to her progeny her independence of mind, her prompt intelligence and will, the sense of humor by which she knew herself. From her, it seems to Andy, had come the quick, elated, untiring intelligence that his father had given to the service of the small farmers of their region. But those qualities, which in his father were usually checked along with his impatience by good sense or a decorum amounting to charity, in his uncle Andrew were allowed to run wild. It was as if Aunt Suzy's attraction to ridicule and ridiculousness, in Uncle Andrew became a compulsion to breach every restraint or boundary that appeared in his way. And so by gleefully and blatantly insulting, one bright summer day, the owner of a .38 pistol, Uncle Andrew obliged himself to depart all at once and forever from Port William and the country around.

That was a truth, hard and immobile, long to learn, for a boy just a month shy of ten years old in the summer of 1944. That a man not evil, who drew friendship and affection to him everywhere he went, could yet turn to his own destruction the overabundant life that made him attractive is a hard fact yet for an old man eighty-four and a half, who has populated the air around him with one of the lineages, incarnate and passing, of the love that so far has seen him through the world.

IV.

When they had eaten dinner and Grandpa, who had been out on horseback all morning, had stoked the fire in the living room and gone to sleep by the stove, and when Andy, who had been watching at the window, saw Dick Watson emerge from his house down by the woods and start up to the barn, he started in a hurry for his coat and cap and overshoes. He was waylaid then by his grandma, who, because his everyday coat that he wore to school was "too good for the barn and the manure and the mud," headed him off and required him to wear her own everyday coat, which embarrassed him by its rolled sleeves, its large glass buttons, and its color, which was more or less purple. But he did not complain. He was in a hurry, and by the time he had got free of the house he had ceased to suffer.

When he came into the barn lot through the yard gate, Dick was just coming through the gate by the loading chute at the opposite corner of the lot. Andy waved, Dick raised his hand in welcome, and Andy started running to make up for time lost. At his age then he was in a hurry to get from the past into the future, and even in overshoes his feet were light. And old Andy remembers, as he watches from what was then the future, that the people he then thought of as "everybody" were still there, still living.

He can see how young and clear he was then by the manner of his greeting to Dick. He did not offer his hand to be shaken, as he would have done had he been older. He did on that day extend his hand, but in the still-surviving habit and candor of his childhood he held it out only to be taken. And Dick took his hand and held it as they walked together to the barn and into it. And in all his being Andy was filled by the happiness of arrival. From town and school, now a long way away, and from a time and times a long time ago, his feet at last were walking on the ground in the only time of the one day that was present. And by holding Dick's hand, that he loved for its hardness and assurance at its work, he felt completed. There was in so fine a moment nothing else that he wanted.

"What are we going to do?"

"Oh, be busy a while, I expect."

"But what?"

"Old boss said to bed the barn. So I expect we're going to bed the barn."

And so, taking a lead rein apiece, they brought the two mules, Beck and Catherine, Dick's team, out of their stalls, offered them water, and hitched them in the driveway beside their stall doors. So far, Dick had let Andy help, as he often would do, because he was glad of the help, or to oblige Andy's unresting wish to be helpful, or both. The question of Andy's standing as a helper and a hand was lively in his mind in those days. And was Dick trusting Beck to him, or trusting him to Beck, who was known as a trustworthy mule?

Once the mules were hitched in their places, Andy had to stand back, as he knew to do. Harnessing a mule was one of the too many tasks for which, as he had been too often informed, he was "too short in the pushup." The lift and carry, for some years yet, were going to be "just a little above his breakfast." Nevertheless, he was now in the place and time and life of the language by which the teamsters talked about harness, which in Andy's home country they called "gear," as they called harnessing "gearing up." Already he had in his mind and mouth the old names that enabled the work he most wanted to do, and he loved the weight and shape of them on his tongue: bridle, headstall, browband, blinders, throatlatch, snaffle bit, hames, hamestrings, hame rings, breast chains, trace chains, backband, belly band, britching, checklines, crosschecks.

When Dick had harnessed the mules, he stood them side by side and fastened the lines and crosschecks to their bits. He stepped behind them, took the lines into his hands, and spoke: "Come up, ladies." And so he began to speak the language, which Andy also knew, and would know and speak to the end of his days as Dick spoke it, by which teamsters talked to their teams: "Come up" and "Gee" and "Haw" and "Whoa" and "Yea back." Those, the most important, but also "Get over" and "Easy" and other things that a teamster's own team (whether he owned them or not) would understand perhaps only when he said them. This language had always the dignity of being necessary, for by it the teamster talked to the team about the work they were doing together, and it gave the pleasure of a sort of singing, for the good teamsters loved to hear themselves speaking it.

Andy following, bringing the two pitchforks they would need, Dick drove the team to the wagon shed, stopped them, turned them, and backed them in, each mule on her side of the tongue. And here was another part of the language that Andy so loved to hear and to speak: tongue, coupling pin, breast chains (another kind), singletrees, doubletree, stay chains. Of all the parts of a wagon, the "hub" of the wheel was the one he had been taught first and most urgently. From the first time he had started to climb into a wagon, he had heard, "Put your foot on the *hub!*" for fear that he would make a ladder of the spokes, which, if the team suddenly started, could get him badly hurt, maybe killed.

As he went about his work, knowing Andy's eagerness to be of use, and wanting anyhow to keep an eye on him, Dick would ask him to help—for instance, to hook Beck's trace chains to her singletree—and would watch to see that he did it right.

That he was Dick's student then and at such times, he *felt*. If asked, he would gladly have acknowledged that Dick taught him things, though he would have hurried to point out that he was not in school and Dick was not a schoolteacher. Only later would he have added, as only later he realized, that he learned from Dick eagerly as, so far, he had learned almost nothing in school.

Only after Dick had driven the wagon out of the shed, out of the lot, and into the pasture behind the barn, because it would have been no use in asking sooner, Andy asked, "Can I drive?"

He was standing, holding to a pocket of Dick's jacket. Dick handed him the lines, and then he steadied himself by resting a hand on Andy's shoulder.

"Watch, now. Mind what you doing."

Of all Andy's admonishers Dick was the quietest, and more apt to warn than correct. The other authorities he answered to were likely to be paying no attention to him until he blundered or offended, and then to deliver overexcited judgments.

Andy drove on into the second field behind the barn, the Middle Field, to what was left of the great stack of barleystraw that had been blown out by Mr. Bruce's threshing machine back in the summer.

As they came up to the stack, Dick took the lines again to position the wagon for loading. Andy's silence then all of a sudden became a silence he had kept since summer. It was about the several hours that he, his brother, Henry, and their friend Fred Brightleaf had spent sliding headfirst down the stack. This his father had sternly forbidden because it scattered and wasted the straw. Overcome by temptation, they had disobeyed, though Andy and Henry knew that their father, driving his car through the fields on one of his tours of inspection, was likely to find them out. The straw they dragged down with them and strewed over the grass could not easily be put back. They had in fact left plenty of evidence, which old Andy knows his father had known, had enjoyed knowing, and was glad he had not caught them. And Andy feels a certain paternal amusement at his father, who then was half his son's age now. In his father's place Andy too would have sternly forbidden, ignored, and enjoyed in thought those long, headfirst, half-falling slides.

Dick handed him a fork and kept one. Then, standing safely apart, they began loosening the straw from the rick and forking it onto the wagon. And Andy was carried motion by motion from his dream of being strong and working well back to the actual boy he was going to be for a good while yet. The fork was mansize, clumsy for a boy. The handle was too long for his height and too big around for his grasp. He blundered and faltered. He still was wavering in the middle of the way between trying to be useful and being useful, the long, ungraced course from trying to work, to learning to work, to working. He would loosen enough straw from the rick to make a forkful, which he would bundle and lift, and too often the slick straw would scatter into the air before he could load it. He would look quickly then to see if Dick had witnessed his defeat.

But Dick was working right along, attending only to his work, and Andy was thus instructed to attend to his own. At least he knew he was being a help. Awkwardly as he was doing it, he was adding bulk to the load. If he was helping at least some, he was free to be happy in being at work with Dick. And he *was* happy, with a large happiness that seemed to him to include everything in sight. When he stopped to rest, as from time to time he needed to do, he could see how well Dick was working. Dick was not hurrying, but was working about exactly as fast as the work needed to be done in order to be done well, and he was keeping his workplace neat. Any straw that he scattered on the ground he gathered, using his fork as lightly as a broom, and tossed it onto the load.

They were working with the help and in the company of what Andy by then was learning to see was a really fine pair of mules that measured up to a pattern carefully formed in the mind of his grandpa. From the height of the ground where they were at work, the whole country lay in the shadowless gray light that touched every grassblade and every straw. The world was all around, and there in the middle of it Dick was so absent from Andy, who was watching, so present in his work, so entirely alive in his life as he was living it, that Andy said to himself as he had heard his father and his grandpa say, usually for his instruction, "Dick knows how to work."

As those words entered his mind, Andy thought, and felt guilty, that he was glad he was at work with Dick and not with his uncle Andrew. If he had been with Uncle Andrew, they would by now have been on the way somewhere else. It would have been a different kind of day, and a kind not as good. Dick was quiet, steady, somehow the same in his being as the being of the world and the day, but Uncle Andrew was loud, unsteady, dedicated wherever he was to somewhere else.

And so Andy was feeling what he could not yet know, but what in his old age, looking back in his tenderness upon that day, he completely knows. While he was there with Dick and the team of mules, trying his poor best to learn a skill and a patience already doomed, he was beginning to awaken in the rift rapidly widening between worlds of two different kinds. One was the world of town and school and automobility, a world forever tilted toward the future that would be always arriving and would never arrive, in which a man like Uncle Andrew could come to rest only by dying. The other world was the one that Andy at that moment stood in, which at that moment was still intact around him. There would be a few more moments and days yet in which he would know its coherence, but it was a world, as he would learn to see, that he had been born barely in time to know, and where for just a little while it still could be known.

Maybe it was a foretaste of a dividing of time that caused Andy to say almost to his surprise, "Dick, if I didn't have to go to school, I could live out here and work with you every day. Wouldn't that be good?"

Dick laughed his laugh of grownup responsibility. "Ho ho ho, now no, buddy. You got to keep in school."

But now that he had heard himself speak his wish, Andy could not easily give it up. "I don't like it. If they didn't make me, I wouldn't go."

"But you got to learn your books. So you can be a lawyer like your daddy. So you can take care of me when I'm old."

This was one of the settled themes of their conversation,

Dick no doubt speaking over Andy's head of a real fear of needing help that he would not have. If Grandpa was in hearing, no doubt knowing Dick's fear in himself, he would vouch for Andy's help. "Ay God, he'll *do* it, Dick."

And so Andy took part in a conversation that he too would come to understand, and the conversation would place itself in time among three old men.

"Ain't we done agreed about that?"

"I said I would. But I'd a lot rather be here with you than in school."

"But you got to go."

Dick said this, Andy thought, with something like sorrow, and so he said no more.

As time would reveal, they both would have to go. Dick departed late in the fall of the next year, his helplessness lasting only hours after he fell in the doorway as he was starting out to work. And the world that he had known would not survive him long.

And Andy, as Dick foresaw, had to go to school. He had to go, after the manner of his kind, and he went until, in his college years, he sometimes went because he wanted to, learned some things he was glad to know, and submitted to the rule of teachers he remembers with love. As Andy lived on from lesson to lesson, year to year, Dick Watson and his ways of doing and the world he belonged to were ever farther behind him, gone, and yet living still in his heart and his thoughts, so that in certain stillnesses of his mind he has continued to see and hear Dick Watson and himself, almost to be with them, as they were.

He has them before him now in the time, one of many he remembers, when they were completing their load of straw to bed the barn. He can see Dick through the boy's eyes with which he saw him then. And because he is also watching from afar, he sees both of them at their work, the motions they made, lighted by the then-passing light now become the light of imagination, in which he sees, clearly as never before, that especially when he worked at his own pace, as he often did, Dick's work was beautiful.

The realization comes as a surprise, and Andy is surprised to be surprised. Perhaps this came so late because as a child he took Dick's work for granted, among much else that was beautiful that he took for granted. Perhaps he had subscribed unconsciously to the latter-day enlightenment that sees the work of Dick's kind, of any race, as "mind-numbing" and so not possibly beautiful. Andy, even so, had long been prepared to see the beauty of it, for he had grown up and lived among farming people who spoke readily of "pretty work." And his early passages through the fields, walking or driving, with his father had included stops, some of them sudden, in the presence of a patch of blooming goldenrod, a flock of sheep at peace, a running fox, a good hand at work: "Beautiful, isn't it."

The sign and signature of the beauty of Dick's work was

that he did not hurry and did not dawdle. He worked at ease. This was a time when it was possible for a lot of people in that country to put their hands to work that was beautiful, and the beauty of their work was of the same kind as all other beauty, leading into time and out of it. The beauty, Andy saw, was a fittingness between Dick and his work, between him and the team he drove and the cows he milked, between him and his life's day and place. It was a fittingness that he had made by the respect he gave to himself and to those things and all things. That fittingness, and his respect that made it, had nothing to do with, and owed nothing to, Grandpa Catlett or anybody else he had ever worked for. It was possible, after all, to pay a man to work and thus to require him to do it, and even, to a point, to do it well, but only by his own choice could he work beautifully. From everybody he had ever worked for, the fittingness and beauty of his work had set him free and made him complete. As a boy, Andy assumed without thinking that when nothing was going wrong, Dick was happy in his work. Old Andy only asks how he could not have been happy if by his own wish and skill he was working beautifully. It seemed sure at least that Dick was more complete than almost everybody Andy would know in the times to come, and the proof simply was that he worked without hurry and did not dawdle. By being skilled and therefore unhurried and beautiful, his work enabled him to live and to last, but also to be pleased, which enabled him to live and to last.

And so it comes plain to Andy, looking back, that in that year of 1944 Dick Watson was the master of a school that neither he nor his student knew they were in. Because of his mastery, the light he had inside him shone around him. And in his presence a boy so critical, so easily dissatisfied, as Andy Catlett then was, could work at learning to work and be quiet.

V.

With Dick working steadily and Andy helping the best he could, they loaded the straw they needed, carried it home, bedded the barn, and put away the mules. And then, because it was too early for the evening chores, they stopped and stood together in the wide-open doorway of the barn, looking out.

This was before the hourly wage had come into the Port William country, and time then, which had the value of life and living, did not yet have a price. People who did nothing because they had nothing to do did not think they were spending time uselessly. Andy's report cards sent home from Hargrave School had a list of scholarly virtues, one of which was "Uses time well," and there might or might not be a check mark in a box beside it. All his life Dick had used his hands and used tools, but he had never thought he was using time. And because he was at the home place, not at school, Andy also was not using time. One of the commonplaces of

his young life, then and for a while longer, when he would accompany Dick and Grandpa Catlett at work, was this coming
to rest when there was nothing to do. If they got done early or
were rained out, they would go and stand, or they would sit
on upturned five-gallon paint buckets, in the doorway of the
barn and look out and talk of the falling rain or of the need
for rain or of other times, or they would find nothing to say
and would say nothing.

In the recovered light of his watching across so many years,
Andy is pleased and reassured to see the two of them merely
standing together, standing still, looking silently out into the
world and the weather: an old black man with a gray mustache, wearing a work jacket tattered and faded and a similarly
historical felt hat, and, no more than a foot from him and
exactly beside him, a small white boy in a too-big purple coat,
with a face as unguarded, as *unmade*, as his life still is. Only
his quietness and his closeness to the old man tell of his happiness in being where he is. They stand still, the two of them,
looking out the door as if to memorize the color of the air.

In the stillness of the old man, as Andy now can see,
there is the weariness of years, which could not be rested
from until, as he sometimes said, there would be in his turn
"slow walking and loud shouting" for him, but also there is
much of patience, and there is a kind of peace, earned and
made, that Andy knows is soon to depart almost entirely
from the country, not soon to return.

The boy's stillness is partly in emulation of the man's and so partly his own, but to the knowing watcher it also is an intimation of the absence of his life yet to come, and of a waiting still as unconscious and unexpecting as that of a seedling tree. His mind, unmade as in itself it still was, was nonetheless being made by the places and companions the world so far had granted him. In times to come, even soon to come, he would know loss and losses, he would live into the absence of great and irreplaceable things uselessly destroyed. He would know much of sorrow. But he would see also much more of the world and its beauty, and of great and beautiful things that humans, uncompleted as they are, have made. He would find, or be found by, the friends and books, the teachers, he would need, often when he most would need them. Love in person, and in persons, would come to him. Happiness would come to him, sometimes for good reasons, sometimes for no reason. He thinks of his good fortune, and his eyes, once so clear and wide, fill with tears.

The two standing in the barn door, at one with the day and their silence, were not prepared for the man who appeared where the driveway curved past the house, and Andy, far more foreknowing now than then, feels still the shock of that appearance. The man seemed to have arrived without approaching, was suddenly there, walking fast and looking around. He was a short man, stoutly made. His face, as sharp and alert as that of a fox, was ill-fitted to the rest of him. He was wearing a canvas hunting coat frazzled and stained, a shapeless felt hat with no band. As he caught sight of the two in the barn door, he hesitated, then nodded his head as if to himself, lifted a hand to them, and came on. Dick opened his hand to Andy, who slipped his hand into it.

For the man was a stranger. Andy had never seen him before. Nor had Dick, as Andy knew from his continued stillness. And then a remarkable thing happened, for the strangeness of this stranger, as if a contagion of himself, made Andy feel that he too was a stranger. After nearly a lifetime, he understands that feeling and still feels it, though by now it is familiar to him. The man's name, he knows, is Legion. He has crossed Andy's path many times, most memorably and often when wearing a suit, and always bearing the contagion of strangeness to whatever part of the world he is in, causing Andy to fear the possibility of such a strangeness in himself, even in his kind.

On that first of his appearances to Andy, the stranger studied him pointedly a moment and then as pointedly disregarded him as of no use.

He turned to Dick. "Say!" It was a command. He was taking control of the situation. He wanted nothing from either of them but what he would ask for.

"Say, old uncle, whose place is this?" He spoke rapidly and decisively in a voice rather high-pitched.

"Mister Marce Catlett's."

"Catlett," the stranger said, acknowledging the existence only of the name, and still looking around with a look that seemed to miss nothing.

"And the road yonder? I'm looking to get to Port William."

"Bird's Branch Road. Yonder's to Port William."

By then Andy knew that Dick was not going to address the stranger as "sir." He was not going to address him as anything. He was not going to tell him more than he was asked for.

"I see," the stranger said, looking about. "I see. Well. All right."

He turned away, revealing something bundled heavily in his coat, making it stick out absurdly behind him. Going then at a half-trot, he was soon past the house and out of sight.

The two in the doorway continued a while to stand without moving or speaking, as if looking at the hole in the air through which the stranger had come and now had gone.

Finally, "He was lost?" Andy said. "What's he doing?"

"Oh, maybe lost," Dick said. "Maybe, maybe not. He's hunting. Running people's traps too, I expect. Seeing everything. You see him looking around? He thinks what anybody's got might as well be his. Ain't no telling what all he's up to."

"There's no limit yet," old Andy thinks. "He's lawless as only a human can be." He feels himself leaning toward them now, reaching out.

Dick was still looking away. To call him back, but also because he wanted to know, Andy asked, "What all's that he's got in his coat?"

"Hides. Game pocket full of hides. Coon, mink, fox, hard to tell. What they could tree and shake out or dig out or take out of somebody's traps. Somebody and a dog or two waiting for him off in the bushes somewhere. Been footing it along the hollows, nights mostly, a good while, I expect. If he was lost that's why. He ain't going to no Port William."

Andy thought of the stranger's snub, first to himself and then to Dick, and he was indignant. "He acted like he didn't know us. Didn't he *know* us?"

"He don't know us," Dick said. "I know him."

Dick was still thoughtfully looking, as if he watched the stranger growing smaller, disappearing at last into the country. And Andy felt his own thoughts drawn away into the folds of the land that now concealed a man there was no telling about. The stranger's strangeness had made Andy aware for the first time of the tenderness and defenselessness of the earth, and a sadness too big for him came upon him. He felt the times of sorrow, the long times, passing like the wind at night over the ridges.

And so he was glad, when his trance released him, to see that he was standing in the barn door, looking across the barn lot and the lot fence at the back of the house, and to find Dick Watson, still standing beside him, still holding his hand.

For the next seventy-five years the flesh of Andy's hand has remembered the hardness, the warmth, and the gentle holding of Dick Watson's hand. "A while longer," he thinks. "For yet a little while." And he gives his thanks.

A Rainbow

(1945–1975–2021)

Several years before he died, before any of us had thought to associate him with a death that might be his, Elton Penn bought the run-down ninety acres directly across the north fork of Bird's Branch from his home place, the Jack Beechum place, that he had come to as a tenant in the spring of 1945 and stayed to own. He bought the ninety acres to redeem his vision of what could be made of it by good treatment. By then Elton had the money to pay for it—and he did value money in proportion more or less to his early want of it—but money in this matter was not his first consideration. His first consideration, which I think he hardly needed to consider, was that he was a farmer born and bred, a land husband, who longed to put his hand to the ground and cause it to flourish. He foresaw the good and beautiful work that would be required to remake what hard use and neglect had unmade, and he wanted to be the one to do it.

This my father understood, for he had done the same

thing, and more than once, for the same reason. That my father had become a lawyer, in addition to the farmer that he, like Elton, was born to be and could never quit being, was because the farm depression of the 1920s so reduced the income to his parents and himself from their own home place that he had to look elsewhere for money. He had been to college, and certain events guided him into law school. That, as it turned out, was in many ways fortunate. It was also one of the anomalies that modern times had begun to impose on our native countryside around Port William.

By necessity, anyhow, my father had two vocations. He was a man, as I saw him early and as I see him now, who most belonged outdoors. Among his right companions would have been a good bird dog, which at least once he had, a well-worked and obliging saddle horse, which he never had, and one of his father's long-outmoded teams of work mules. And so his office was for him often enough a place of exile. And yet he found in the law also a true calling. He loved his knowledge of it. He reveled in it. And yet at the end of the day when he shut his office door and headed out of town into the wide world where his cattle were grazing, he was a man going home. Some of his days would also begin with farming: a quick trip after breakfast to see what had happened during the night, to do something that needed doing that would not wait until evening, or just to allow, while he could, an unbounded space to enter his mind.

My father was Wheeler Catlett. His father, Marce Catlett, and Jack Beechum, two of the old kind, had lived as neighbors, their farms on opposite sides of the road. As a lawyer, my father had inherited Old Jack as a client, just as Old Jack laid claim to my father as a possession in consideration of time and interest invested in him and his upbringing from about the time my father learned to walk. And so it was my father, who had looked up Elton, on the recommendation of Braymer Hardy, to be Old Jack's tenant in his declining years. "He's a good one," Braymer told my father, who took him at his word. He knew Braymer as an elder who seemed appointed to keep watch for "a good one" of whatever kind, who was more than apt to know what a good one was, and to know what he was looking at when one appeared. "He'll take hold," Braymer said. "He'll do."

And Elton, who stood up fully to Braymer's measure, stood up also to Old Jack's. He became in effect Old Jack's son and in more than one way his heir. Half-orphaned in his childhood by the death of his father, Elton was crowded to the outer edge of his mother's household and care, and finally out of the house itself when he was fourteen, by an unkind stepfather. And then, four years later, to complete his singling out from lives he might possibly have lived, and to place him in the life he would have, the one he resolutely did live for the next thirty-six years, he was disowned with his young wife by her parents.

Elton, as they saw him, came from nothing. He was of low birth and circumstances. He possessed eight grades of schooling, a team of horses, a few tools, and the knowledge of the use of them, but no visible prospects, no "future." He was no doubt as far as possible unlike the minister or the doctor the lofty Mountjoys had foreseen and spoken for as their son-in-law. But by the time he was twenty-five he had within him, nevertheless, a settled love of farming and an ability to work and manage that were rare and plain enough to have attracted the discerning eye of Braymer Hardy.

And so Elton came to the Beechum place with something of a reputation and was so far explained, but to a further extent he came unexplained—as, to a further extent, probably all of us do. His father had been a hard, capable worker, and a renowned teamster who, as Braymer told it, "when he was saw-logging in the woods, could make one horse stand and the other one pull, and never touch a line." But Elton was only nine years old when his father died, and so what he got from his father must have come partly by example and some instruction, partly from what he overheard. He told me once of his father's precaution against harness galls when he was working his horses hard in hot weather: "When he stopped to let them rest, he would raise their collars and piss on their shoulders." This was a practice well known and often followed by the oldtime teamsters. It is another testimony to his father's horsemanship.

But mostly Elton's inheritance from his father was within him when he was born.

Though Elton blamed his mother for the encroachment of her too-soon-married second husband, he also spoke of her with carefully weighed respect. His gift for management—for rightly ordering his workdays and his work, his place and the seasons—certainly might have come from her. He remembered a dry year, probably 1930, when their garden did not make. When its failure was clear and complete, his mother made one trip to the store, bought all the canned goods she perfectly knew they would need until the next year's garden, and she never went back to the store. When Elton was still a dependent boy, she bought him a pair of brown cotton gloves at the start of every winter. If he lost them, he got no more. If he kept them, she would mend and patch them endlessly to make them last until spring, and he remembered his pride in the beautiful care she gave to her stitches.

"He don't come from nothing," Braymer told my father. "But nothing is pret' near what he'll bring with him. He's got a good enough pair of horses and a milk cow—paid for, I think—some chickens, a few tools. And I'd say he's married to a right good girl."

"That's something," my father said. "Enough, maybe."

"Enough for a start," Braymer said. "There'll be more. That old place he's started out on don't amount to much. It's held him back. Put him on a good farm—put him on that old Beechum place that's been looked after—it'll be something to see."

It was something to see. Elton came to the Beechum place with Mary, his wife, with the few animals, tools, and household furnishings they had managed so far to own, with his intelligence and talent, his athlete's grace and dexterity at his work, but also, and above all, the passion with which he used his gifts, his so far cooped-up desire to farm, his quickness in possessing everything he learned, his delight in the use of his mind.

The Beechum place, in a way, set him free. It gave him scope, room to reach out with his mind and his hands to see how much he could do of what might be done. In the first year and often enough in the years that followed, he worked in a kind of elation. In that first spring, once he had made his own beginning at the beginning of the crop year, he began to leave behind him the visible marks and signs by which he would be known. Everywhere he worked he made order. Task by task, piece by piece, he began to recover the Beechum place from the inattention that had come upon it in Old Jack's waning years. It seemed to turn back toward life. It seemed to come again into sight and to be seen. It began to look, as Elton himself said, "like somebody *lives* here."

My father saw that this was so. He told Braymer, "You were right about him."

And Braymer said, "Wheeler, you don't need to tell that to *me*."

A RAINBOW

My grandfather Catlett, watching from across the road, saw that it was as Braymer had said it would be. Old Jack saw it. Eventually, so did I. And so, from watching Elton, from working for him as a hired hand, finally from working with him as his neighbor and friend, I came, like Braymer Hardy, to know a good one when I saw one.

We arrive here in this world having forgotten where we came from, though something of a memory seems to remain: a whisper, a distant shine like that of a house window at night on the far side of the valley, perhaps what some have called "the inner light," to guide us when finally we have been jolted awake. And so we don't come from nothing. But once here we don't know where we are. At first I learned the world as a book written, completed the day before my birth, not to be changed by another penstroke. And then I saw that some I knew were departing from it, never to return, and new strangers were arriving. The newcomers, if they stayed, would learn more or less of where they were. And then, in time, they too would depart, taking with them the sum of all they had learned, leaving behind them maybe a few who would remember them, and then the rememberers too would go and be gone. I see in this the order of things, nothing to complain about. I have been here long enough to watch the whole turn of the wheel. I see that we are passing through this world like a river of water flowing through a river of earth. A far cry from a written book, the world—to extend my desperate metaphor—is a book ceaselessly being written, and not in a human language. This too has not been submitted to our judgment, and it is not for us to regret. To give thanks seems truly to be the right response, for as we come and go we learn something of love, the gift and the giving of it, and this appears to lay a worth upon us, if we want it, if we accept it, to give us standing hereafter.

That is the heart speaking in the heart's language, and out of a mystery so vast that order and chance may be reconciled within it. Because, for all we surely know, we come into our times and places as much at random as leaves falling, it is remarkable, as I look back, that Elton seems to have stepped at the age of twenty-five into vacancies in the story of our home country that had been devised for him, for which he had been predestined and prepared. As he entered into his life on the Beechum place, as if according to nature so that probably none of us saw it happening, he became Old Jack's appointed son and successor, my grandfather Catlett's neighbor and student, my father's student and friend, my friend and teacher. He went among us in his way of always paying attention, learning us, making of us and for us and to us a sense that, without him, we could not have made for ourselves. His sense of us gave us a sort of historical coherence, in which of course he himself was included.

As everybody saw soon enough, Mary was the "right good girl" Braymer had said she was. She was to the end of his days the help meet for him that Elton would always need. She made him the only household and home that ever was securely his. And she loved him. When necessary, she worked beside him in the field. She often cooked dinner, by herself, for a dozen hands and then, as soon as she had done the dishes, went to work with the crew she had fed. And I remember her avowal of Elton's advantage in the bad weather of the seasons and his moods: "*He* had *me*."

Young as they were, so distinguished as they were by their orphan marriage, the notoriety and the hurt of it, Elton and Mary seemed to make a sort of refuge of my Catlett grandparents, to whom they endeared themselves by being young and well-mannered and glad to help. In the afternoons, when she was caught up in her work, Mary often would walk across the fields to visit with my grandmother, from whom she took comfort and learned a lot and borrowed books, and whom she called "Grandma," as I did. And often in the evenings Mary and Elton would drive over in their car, a mudstained and hard-used black coupe, to sit and talk until bedtime.

Elton, who was eager to prove himself and was watchful for any advantage, had not been long on the Beechum place before he bought a secondhand tractor, large for the time, with cleated iron wheels. His purpose was to add some custom work for neighbors to his own work at home. Because the tractor was equipped with lights, he could do a good deal of the extra work at night. His only head-on confrontation with my grandfather came when he drove the tractor into the barn lot at our home place early one morning, intending only to take what really was a reasonable shortcut to a neighboring farm where he was going to work. But the tractor's loud exhaust brought my grandfather out of the barn with his cane in the air. "Nawsir! Nawsir! Get that God damned thing *out* of here!"

Elton killed the engine. "How're you this morning, Mr. Catlett!"

"I don't want that thing on this place!" The old man's voice was shaking. "It's got no *business* here! It don't *belong* here!"

"Yessir!" Elton said. "I pretty well know what you mean." In fact, and all of a sudden, he pretty well did know. He had felt his heart touched by my grandfather's passion. He sat on his high seat, looking down at my grandpa, who seemed to have come rushing out of a time before that time, and who stood with his cane still raised as if to kill the tractor by striking it on one of its vital parts, and whose eyes shone with a hard blue light. And Elton felt himself, to his surprise, on the verge of a radical beginning he was not altogether glad of. He did still love and was proud of the horses that for a while he would still be using—his seasoned team, Prince and Dan, and the green-broke three-year-old he called Dobbin—and he knew Marce Catlett's reputation as a mule man and a teamster. But the morning light was still brightening and he was on his way to

work. Also he was amused, in fact delighted. He had been smiling when he spoke, and he was still smiling, because the circumstances asked him to do so, also because he could not stop.

"Uncle Marce," he said, giving him the customary honor
of his old age, "I was hoping you wouldn't mind if I drive
across your place to get to Mr. Simms's. That'll get me to
work a little quicker."

"Simms's! You got no work at home?"

"Plenty. But I'm pretty well caught up over there. I'm going to do some plowing for Mr. Simms. Some other people
too. I'd like mighty well to get ahold of some money."

"Money! What do you need with money?"

"Well, I wouldn't mind having some, but it's the fellow
over at the bank that's needing it." He was not going to say
that he had got the loan to pay for the tractor.

"You owe money at the bank, boy?"

"Yessir. Mr. Wheeler Catlett has stood behind me for a
loan. I want to get it paid."

Elton knew he had been coming to judgment. He would
remember that my grandfather's eyes had become thoughtful
instead of angry, though they kept a hard glitter. He was still
looking at Elton, the cane still raised but apparently forgotten.

"Yes!" he said. "Pay if off! Stay out of debt if you can. It'll
ruin you. I know what I'm talking about."

He turned a little aside then, as if only to let himself
think, and for a while neither of them spoke.

"I've lived here all my life. Or mighty near all of it. Most of it under the burden of owed money. A time was I asked too much of my place. I made some mistakes. I've mended it back the best I could. I'd hate to see it trampled by that thing, with debt driving it."

Elton said not a word. He had heard his fear speaking.

"But mainly I've treated it right. You can look at it and see what you think."

And then an ache of understanding startled Elton's heart. It seemed to him that he became older.

"Mr. Catlett," he said. They were looking at each other then, and Elton's voice and my grandfather's had come into accord. "I have looked. And I know what to think."

"We were sounding alike," Elton would say when he told this story, which he loved and told many times, to me, to my brother, to anybody listening—and of course always to himself, to test his understanding.

"Boy," my grandfather said, "you had your shoes on before daylight," and this was merely a statement.

"Yessir."

"And it'll likely be dark again before you pull 'em off."

"I expect it will."

Some more thinking then was done, and Elton waited.

"You were aiming to drive through here to get over to Simms's."

"Yessir."

"To break ground for old man Simms."

"Yessir."

"To get money to pay to the bank."

"Yessir."

"And when you go through my gates, you'll fasten 'em behind you."

"Yessir, Mr. Catlett, I will."

And then, while the tractor's steering wheel itched under Elton's right hand, my grandfather looked into him at a place, Elton said, where everything he had ever done "was written in writing."

When my grandfather was satisfied with his reading, he appeared to remember the cane, which he had lowered and now raised again, this time in a kind of salute.

"Son, you're all right. You're a good one. Drive on."

After that, and during the time, almost a year, they were allowed to live and speak as neighbors, you might say that Elton made an effort to memorize my grandfather. To an extent that was significant certainly for me, he succeeded. He was a good student of character, who had always paid close attention to his elders. He had watched Braymer Hardy, for instance, as carefully as Braymer had watched him. He had made no big thing of his watching, but he saw that Braymer was, in his entirely unpresuming way, a superior man. Just by keeping interested, Elton had picked up the character, the feeling, the tone or the tune, of Braymer's way of being in the world. So he did with my grandfather, whom he often quoted to me. Sometimes this would be a handing on of advice: "See, laugh, and say nothing"—by which my grandfather refused standing to what he thought unworthy. Sometimes, just for his delight in it, Elton would repeat: "Son, you're all right. You're a good one. Drive on." He did not mimic my grandfather, but he did deliver rightly the gravity and tone and emphasis of my grandfather's sayings as they would be brought to mind. When in remembrance and commendation he would repeat to me, "Ay God, son, I know what a man can do in a day," the tone of his voice would tell me how, in my grandfather's understanding, that knowledge could be both exultant and tragic. To a man eager and strong a day is an invitation, but the day passes, and in passing it sets upon his mind and his hands its intractable limit.

And so Elton was able to convey to me my grandfather himself as I remembered him. But he also gave me a competent appraisal and sense of my grandfather's worth, the tone or tune of his experience of this world, that I could not have received for myself when I was a boy. I am more completely my grandfather's grandson than I would have been had Elton not so carefully known us.

In the same way, he completed my sonship to my father. That was because he and my father, in a way that was crucial

to them both, completed each other. The two of them knew
nobody, had no friend, as much in love with farming, so un-
endingly interested in it, so eager to talk about it, as they
were. They spent countless Sunday afternoons driving in my
father's car over their farms, slowly, contemplatively, often
stopping, looking at the crops, the pastures, and the livestock, noticing qualities, likenesses and differences, also just
keeping company with each other, remembering things, telling stories, laughing. Of all that our land produced in those
days, their greatest love and interest went to the pastures and
the grazing animals. The sight of good cattle or good sheep
on good pasture could stop them even from talking. I know
this because from my boyhood until I was more or less one
of them, I would be sitting in the back seat, listening. That
conversation that they carried on in my father's sequence of
scratched and scarred Chevrolets, considering the variety of
its subjects and the ardor and care with which they were dis-
cussed, was the best part of my education, and the part I loved
best because none of us thought it "educational." Only long
into the absence of those friends have I thought how badly I
have sometimes reduced them by calling them my teachers.
Each of them at times did deliberately and pointedly teach
me. But mostly they taught me by example and by the good
chance that made me their overhearer, at times when they
thought of me only when I was needed to open a gate.

My father thought Elton "the best manager of work" he

had ever known and gave full respect to his mind. Elton, who was an equal partner in their friendship, nevertheless studied my father with full appreciation of the rarity he happened to be in his place and time. One day when my father was showing his cattle to a prospective buyer, Elton rode along in the back seat, in my role as observer, auditor, and gate-opener. The cattle were scattered somewhat widely, and as my father drove his car among them, Elton said, he never approached one of them from a slant or angle that did not show it to advantage. "He was *thinking*," Elton said to me, whose mind was still young and wandering, "*all* the time."

He told me some things also that I would never have heard from my father. They went, just the two of them, on a bird-hunting trip down south, I forget where. On their way home in the dark of an evening, my father was driving fast, and they were intently talking. They came upon a curve in the road that was too sharp for their speed, as my father saw too late. It was a left-hand curve. On the right-hand side of the road, just at the start of the curve, a farm gate was standing wide open. Braking carefully and still talking, my father drove through the gate into what the headlights revealed to be a fairly level pasture. He had done a lot of what we now call "off-road driving." He often had avoided getting stuck in unpaved places, and seldom, but often enough, had got stuck. And so he felt equal to the present emergency, made perfectly confident by so much imperfect experience.

Without slowing down more than enough, exactly preserving the needed momentum, still talking, he made a long, gentle loop out into the pasture, drove once more through the gate and back again onto the road. They had been talking about the right time to sow red clover. When he first had applied his brakes, my father was remembering one of the half a dozen old farmers he had prized as clients because they knew so much. Mr. Buttermore. Like Elton, I had heard my father speak of Mr. Buttermore.

"Mr. Buttermore," my father said, "always sowed red clover in November."

"Your daddy never stopped talking," Elton said.

"And," my father said, "he may have been right."

"Your daddy," Elton said, "had got started and he wasn't finished."

For all the good, and also the goodness, that Elton had in him, he was not an easy man. Because of the hard circumstances of his life after his father's death, the never-ended antagonism between him and his stepfather, the rejection of his and Mary's marriage by her parents, he came to the Beechum place bearing more than his share of anger and resentment. Though this was perfectly understandable and so (by some) forgivable, it could make him extremely touchous. He could be hard to get along with. He disliked a lot of people. The insult he received from his self-exalted in-laws was a sting he felt for many years. It was a wound deliberately given, and it was grossly unjust. But Elton also was much inclined, as my father put it, "to cherish petty grievances," about which he could be fiercely outspoken.

My father, as sympathetic and generous as he could be, and often was, also was not an easy man. He was quick-minded, which shortened his patience. When he was wound up in certain ways, he could be peremptory and regardless, about as tactful as a handsaw. And so the way between him and Elton was not always smooth. They would fall out, not so far as I know for any reason very large or significant, but there would be some negligence, a disappointment, a fancied slight. "We both," Elton once said, "are as sensitive as your eye." They were not so petty as to not-speak or turn their backs. But there would be times when they did not see much of each other. And then whatever their difference had been would wear out or disappear, and they would take up where they had left off. I think that few friends have been so nearly of one mind about the things that mattered to them both.

Years ago, when I was still in my teens and was working for Elton in the tobacco cutting, one of my fellow harvest hands was Floyd Moneyworth, known as Fatty. Fatty was not fat, but he had been somewhat plump when he was a boy, which had been a distinction, a rare thing in those days. Perhaps contradicting Fatty's surname, Elton refused to pay his earned wages in full until the harvest was over. That was for fear that Fatty, while he was still needed, would be drawn back into the daytime portion of the Port William conversation, of which he was a hereditary member, and from which he had solemnly agreed with Elton to take a temporary leave of absence.

One day when the two of us were working side by side, Fatty confided to me: "They're saying you've got an old head." By "they" he meant the elders and authorities of the conversation, which for the time being he was attending only between suppertime and bedtime, and into which he evidently had inserted the members of our crew. By "old head" I believe I thought then that he and they meant that my mind was more serious or settled, less threatening, less potentially dangerous, than the minds of some other big boys. Until just now I had not for a long time remembered Fatty and his handing over to me the revelation that I had an old head. I suppose that phrase, that concept, has come back to me now because now I finally need it.

The phrase may well have meant what I at first thought it did. But the world changes, perspective lengthens, and that was seventy years ago. My mind now is not as superficial as it was then. And now I hold the minds of the elders and authorities of old Port William in far more respect than I did then. I am one of them now, one of the last of them. I know how much they had known of time and change, how much and how well some of them had thought about what they knew, how well some of them remembered what they would rather have forgot. I know that they knew then more about my family and history, more about me, than I did. And ever since I had got big enough to walk about on my own among the town's sitting and talking places, they had been watching me, teasing me, sometimes befriending and indulging me. They knew things about me that I had not yet noticed or, as a chuckleheaded big boy, had for the time being forgot or thought I had outgrown: that I was a listener and a watcher, that I could be so intent and quiet on the edge of their conversation that they would forget I was there, that I liked the company of the old people.

I am able now to imagine that they regarded me as a throwback, a boy from somewhere back in their time, who had somehow turned up in my time. And so, I imagine, they may have thought of me as something like a late-come contemporary of theirs: a young boy with an old head. At the time of that crop year, 1950 or a little later, I had updated myself into an authentic chucklehead who thought my driver's license more liberating than the Bill of Rights. But there had been a time before that when in a sort of elation—sometimes in prepared speeches to my more indulgent elders—I had imagined what would be made of me by the ownership of a team of mules, a wagon, and some tools. After that there had been a time when in solitude, understanding by then my oddity, I had mourned the displacement by tractors of the living creatures bred and born to work. This grief was less a thought than a feeling, a sort of palpable emptiness in the mysterious organ, both bodily and cultural, that we call "the heart." For after all I had seen with my own eyes the way a grown man could be completed, even improved, by the collaboration between himself and a good team of mules—not in that way so different from the collaboration between a hunter and a good dog, which also I had seen.

And so it has occurred to me that Elton and my father must have belonged before me to the rare company of people with old heads, for I knew that they hearkened back to older times and ways, and that the landmark by which the three of us had oriented ourselves to our home country and to one another had been Marce Catlett, my grandfather. What young man other than Elton could have looked down from the tall perch of his first tractor at that outraged old man and understood him, felt for him, and in fact loved him? And my father, having begun his passage back across the threshold of this world, in one of his mind's final clarities, spoke of his father: "We miss him, don't we?"

It must have been because we knew collectively my grandpa Catlett, because we saw and recognized in him some determination we might otherwise not have known in ourselves, we were moved by an old feeling in the bones, an old delight in the places of this world that we needed to live in, work in, know the light and the weather in, to the end of our days. The sympathy, the unanimity, that passed among us remains with me in their absence, and it will remain with me, I pray, as a consolation and a light as long as I am here.

In the decades between Elton's arrival on the Beechum place and his death, it seems to me now that the three of us were working out the terms of a fittingness to our home country here and so to one another. That fittingness, so far as it was made, I had to grow up into, for I was the youngest, the slowest, and certainly the most distracted. After I came to it, it became simply necessary to my mind's way of knowing itself and locating itself. And when I settled here at home and made the old-headed choice of a team of horses to do my farming, who were my most eager encouragers and abettors but Elton and my father?

But significant and dear as our understanding has been, it has had to be maintained by much resistance to all that has been brought upon the world by the geniuses of greed, conquest, and war. As we lived and went on, anomalies continued to gather around us: things which were alien to the life and intelligence of this place, but which for us, in our time and times, were inescapable. We were living into the ever-greatening domination of the land and the people by machines.

Though this was entirely materialistic and the work of materialists, it was the ascendancy of mind over matter, giving to thought an absolutely logical or mechanical propulsion toward the disembodiment of human life. It imposed on the living land and people an economy merely mental, merely an idea, that steadily ruled and diminished the lives of both. Elton, in his time, saw and foresaw much of this. My father, who survived Elton by seventeen years, saw more of it—saw it in fact established, temporary as it has got to be, as the only way of the world. I, who now have survived my father by thirty years, have seen its triumph, as if in their exiled millions the people have unanimously lifted their feet from the land and washed the stain of it from their shoes.

Elton, who in the spring of 1945 drove into Grandpa Catlett's barn lot under his curse and left with his blessing, drove on into the time determined to come, that my grandfather could not have imagined or believed. Elton had begun a succession of tractors that would carry him from the clear advantage offered by the first one to a young man, strong and tireless, who wanted to plow at night, to his last one that, as he saw, was a part of the progression toward the even larger machines that would cost too much and earn too little.

Those Sunday afternoon conversations in my father's automobile, which were and are so dear to me, were powered by oil and fire, and were more ominous than we could then have known. And yet, convergent as it was upon the time to come, that conversation was an inheritance. It descended to us from Grandpa Catlett, a somewhat tragic figure, lonely in his marriage, the last of those we called "the old kind," who stood behind us even as we departed from him. We would never know again in our country a man so intact, so fully incarnate as he was, who had never enlarged himself by a power that he had not spoken to and been heard by.

The ninety-acre place across the creek, that late in his life Elton bought and called simply "Across the Creek" or "Over Yonder," he meant to use as winter pasture for his brood cows. He would mow it early for hay and then let the grazing accumulate until cold weather, when he would move the cows over there to make and birth their calves. To shelter the cattle and to store the hay he needed to supplement the pasture, he built a barn that after half a century is still standing.

He spent a lot of time in thinking about and designing the barn, drawing the plan of it in ruled lines, revising and perfecting it as his thoughts changed and improved. To build it he had lumber milled from big trees cut on the place. I regretted without saying so the sacrifice of the trees, but I also saw how appropriate it was that the cattle should thus be sheltered by the land that fed them.

The barn stood for Elton's good will toward the animals that depended on him as he depended on them. It was stoutly built, with a shed roof, its open side facing away from the prevailing winds, offering shelter to the cows when they would be most in need. The barn embodied Elton's kindness to them—his thanks, you might say—his comfort in their comfort. It was his watchfulness over them paid in advance.

The barn, I think, also embodied Elton's love for good work: work good in the moment it was being done, as he did it, and then a lasting good. "Don't think of the dollar, think of the job," he would say, meaning that if you kept your mind on your work and did it right, maybe you wouldn't need to worry about the dollar. This was the law of an ancient love, passing from the world, but he kept it alive in himself, and he taught it to me.

The injured land, by his use of it, healed and became better. It looked better. "It looks like somebody *lives* there," he would say, and he would laugh.

In his own latter years and while he was still an active participant in this world, my father from time to time would remember something or discover something that he would want to show me. He would drive in at my place, going slow, considering, looking around. When I came outside to meet him or he came upon me at work, he would lean across the seat, unlatch the passenger side door, and push it open. "Come go with me." It was not an order, for by then it did not occur to him that I might not do as he told me. Which I did joyfully, for at those times, when he was glad to see me and full of the sense of adventure, he was excellent company, and I would be comforted to be with him.

One warm rainy afternoon in the second spring after Elton died, while we were still getting used to his absence, my father drove over to get me. "Come go with me." He had located the site of an old grist mill of which he knew some history, and he wanted us to look at it together.

The ruins of the mill were in the valley of a large creek that empties into the Ohio River west of Hargrave. My father stayed on his marks and drove directly to it. We examined the disintegrating stone walls of the mill itself and then walked for some distance along the mill race that had been dry and grass-covered for many years.

The mill had been built at the start of the white people's occupation of that valley. The mill race we were walking in had been dug by Indians whom the miller and others had enslaved and put to work under threat of death. As those men, supposedly wild, were completing what was supposedly a first work of domestication, the chief of the enslaved Indians appeared on the bluff above them and hurled down a curse upon the miller and upon all of his get that might survive him in that place.

The story, as my father knew it and told me, is far from

complete. It tells the origin of the mill race, and it remembers the chief's curse by remembering also that, for as long as the miller and his family lasted there, they suffered one dire misfortune after another. My father knew the rules of evidence. He knew the differences between proof and coincidence and between truth and belief. He had applied his mind for years to the sense of the words "deserve" and "deserving." There was a certain standing he could not grant to the chief's curse as the cause of the miller's fate. But he did grant fully the gravity and magnitude, the historical sense and portent, of the coincidence, if that is what it was. And so, in his telling, the story was weighted by his acknowledgment that we had behind us a door remaining ajar, that we might shut and lean against, but could not latch.

We went on and stopped again at an abandoned house and farmstead that my father also knew the history of and wanted to see. He remembered it from many years ago when it was a flourishing small place. Now the house showed the bad signs of use by people who did not live there, or perhaps not anywhere. In the barn we found still hanging on its pegs the set of harness worn by that farm's last team of mules. The leather was dry and cracked, the hardware crusted with rust. We rode on from there several miles without thinking of anything we wanted to say.

Our windings pretty soon took us onto the river road from Hargrave to Port William. My father speeded up a little. I thought he was ready then to take me home. But he soon turned into the lower end of the Bird's Branch road and began the climb out of the river valley, following through the woods and along the creek the road that would take us up onto the open ridge, past Elton's place and our home place.

The weather had become more unsettled. There had been showers, starting and stopping, passing over quickly, divided by big patches of blue sky. When we came up out of the hollow onto the ridge, we were in sunlight, but a large dark cloud had piled up on the horizon in the west. An extraordinarily brilliant rainbow had formed over there, the secondary bow almost as bright as the other. The great double arc appeared to stand just beyond Elton's Across-the-Creek place. At the entrance into that place, my father abruptly, as his way was, turned in, drove over the cattle guard, and on back to the barn, which was almost centered beneath the rainbow. Within the inmost arc there was an intense golden light.

My father lifted his foot from the accelerator, let the car roll to a stop, turned off the engine, and let his hand fall open onto his knee. We seemed then to be inside the light. Neither of us moved or spoke. The light seemed almost substantial, ambient and directionless as a still mist that is almost rain, too light to fall. It seemed to touch everything and to perfect everything it touched.

We sat perfectly still, for what I believe we both thought an allotted time. We understood that this would happen to us only once. It might happen again, but we would not be there together to see it. We knew that we could not remain in that beautiful light. We needed to go before it was gone, so as not to spoil it by our too much wanting.

I was not surprised but was nonetheless glad when my father reached forward and touched the key.

"Well," he said, and it was a benediction. "If Elton sees it now, he's pleased."

Acknowledgments

Of the stories in this book, "One Nearly Perfect Day" and "How It Went" were first published by *The Sewanee Review*; "A Conversation," "A Time Out of Time," "One of Us," "Dismemberment," "The Great Interruption," "The Branch Way of Doing," "The Art of Loading Brush," "A Time and Times and the Dividing of Time," and "A Rainbow" by *The Threepenny Review*; and "A Clearing" by *The Hudson Review*; and of course I am grateful to those magazines for the kindness and the room that they have given me.

I am grateful also to Tanya Berry, who helped these stories by her investment in them of her interest, attention, good judgment, love, and several kinds of work; to my dear and patient friend David Charlton, who made computer copies of these stories, and then, in the pauses of an ongoing conversation also necessary to me, helped me to make large, small, and innumerable revisions; to Wendy Lesser, editor of *The Threepenny Review*, whose resistance, fully clarified, was

ACKNOWLEDGMENTS

indispensable to the longest of these stories; to Gray Zeitz and Leslie Shane of Larkspur Press, who gave to two of these stories, "The Great Interruption" and "One of Us," the distinction of their friendship and their beautiful work; to Lynn Telleen, editor of *The Draft Horse Journal*, who continued my happy association with that magazine by reprinting "One Nearly Perfect Day"; to Janet Renard, who, as copy editor, helped these stories by her surpassing care, good sense, and kindness; and to Jack Shoemaker, my friend inside and outside Counterpoint, for everything.

© Guy Mendes

WENDELL BERRY, an essayist, novelist, and poet, has been honored with the T. S. Eliot Prize, the Aiken Taylor Award for Modern American Poetry, the John Hay Award of the Orion Society, and the Dayton Literary Peace Prize Richard C. Holbrooke Distinguished Achievement Award, among other distinctions. In 2010, he was awarded the National Humanities Medal by President Barack Obama, and in 2016, he was the recipient of the Ivan Sandrof Life Achievement Award from the National Book Critics Circle. Berry lives with his wife, Tanya Berry, on their farm in Henry County, Kentucky.